The Fury of Iron Eyes

The infamous bounty hunter known as Iron Eyes finally manages to catch up with outlaw Dan Creedy and faces him down. With his usual deadly resolve and impeccable aim, Iron Eyes would have dispatched Creedy and claimed the reward. Yet this time it was different for, at last, he had met a man who was almost his equal.

Like an injured animal seeking a place to die, the seriously wounded Iron Eyes rides off towards the forest. But little does he know that the forested hills are part of the reservation belonging to the Southern Cheyenne. He encounters a young Indian hunter called Silent Wolf and the two become friends.

But suffering from horrific blood loss, Iron Eyes has no idea that Dan Creedy's three outlaw brothers are now hunting him.

For the first time in his life, it is Iron Eyes who is the prey. . . .

The Fury of Iron Eyes

RORY BLACK

A Black Horse Western

ROBERT HALE · LONDON

Typeset by
Derek Doyle & Associates, Liverpool.
Printed and bound in Great Britain by
Antony Rowe Limited, Wiltshire

Dedicated to my friend Stuart Wall

PROLOGUE

Since the first man walked upon the land which has come to be known as America, there have been legends. Tales of men blessed or perhaps cursed by the Great Spirit.

One such legend still thrives throughout the cultures of the people known as Native Americans. But even long ago, when a thousand tribes were scattered across the land that stretches from sea to shining sea, this legend was said to be true.

For there are those who are said to be able to change into creatures of the plains and forest as well as the sky. Men who somehow can transform their entire being into that of an eagle or a bear, a buffalo or a deer.

Some it is claimed, can actually become wolves.

Whatever the truth of these stories, it must be said that even today, in various corners of the land that once entirely belonged to the various

7

tribes of Indian, this belief is still harboured by even the most intelligent of souls.

What would the infamous bounty hunter, known only as Iron Eyes, make of a young Cheyenne hunter who claimed that he was one of that rare breed who could turn themselves into a wolf?

Perhaps if Iron Eyes had not been terribly injured when he encountered the handsome Indian, he might have dismissed the claim as nothing more than a brash boast from the lips of a youth trying to impress an elder.

But there was something about the little hunter that made the infamous Iron Eyes consider the claim seriously. Something that made him feel that this was not idle boasting but perhaps, the truth.

There were and still are many legends in the vast land known as America. Tales that span the entire continent. To dismiss any of them out of hand, might seem sensible to the well educated amongst us, but to those who are actually intelligent, it might just be wise to consider them seriously for more than a fleeting moment.

Iron Eyes instinctively knew that the little hunter, called Silent Wolf, was unlike any other person he had ever encountered during his many blood-stained years.

Perhaps the handsome little hunter *could* actually change himself into a wolf. Iron Eyes knew that only time would tell.

ONE

Night had come swiftly to the small, acrid-smelling town of Bonny, Northern Texas. Yet even as darkness overwhelmed the dry, weathered structures, it grew no cooler than it had been when the merciless sun blazed down from the cloudless sky.

The stench of a dozen outhouses hung on the evening air as the gaunt rider aimed his lathered-up mount at the array of wooden buildings. A blind man could have found this town by following his nose, but this rider was not blind. His bullet-coloured eyes had followed the tracks in the almost virginal sand by day and night to this place, because his prey was here, and he was and always had been above all things, a hunter.

Coyotes bayed across the barren range, as if trying to see which could make the loudest noise to greet the large, orange moon that rose above the desolate landscape. But the rider did not seem to hear the wild, doglike creatures as he dug his razor-sharp spurs into the sides of his exhausted horse. For this rider, there was only one thing which mattered: that was cornering the man he sought, and then killing him.

As the smell grew stronger in the flared nostrils of the silent man, he reined in and stood in his stirrups, watching the sleepy town a mere mile ahead.

The light from a solitary saloon was all the illumination within the boundaries of Bonny, but it was enough. It bathed the single street between the wooden buildings in an almost amber light as it spewed from the open saloon doorway. The sound of a tinny piano drifted on the warm air into the ears of the bounty hunter as he rested his pitifully thin frame back down on to the saddle. Even in the moonlight, the face of the rider seemed to hail from another world; a world where skeletons must live to take the lives of men. His face was scarred by many years and many battles. His matted long hair hung limply to his shoulders and flapped like the wings of a bat whenever a breeze dared to touch it. Slowly, his long fingers dragged a thin black cigar from one of his deep jacket pockets before placing it between his small sharp teeth.

Striking a match, Iron Eyes lifted the flame to

the end of the cigar and dragged the strong smoke
into his lungs, holding it there long enough for it
to take effect. He had not eaten anything in two
days as he had followed the trail left by the man
he hunted, yet felt no hunger pangs in his emaci-
ated frame.

Other men ate two, three or even four times a
day, but not Iron Eyes. He had lived too long out
in the wilderness of this great land and ate like
all hunters: only when he had trapped and killed
his prey.

There was an excitement inside the man as he
inhaled the smoke of his cigar and studied the
distant town. Iron Eyes had always grown excited
as he closed in on his prey and readied himself for
the kill. It had started long ago when he had
hunted only animals and even now, as he tracked
men for the price on their heads, the thrill was
still there.

Many thought the strange, tall bounty hunter
was devoid of any emotion whatsoever, but it was
not true. Iron Eyes could not have lived so long
without the sheer passion that drove him on and
on in his pursuit of those wanted dead or alive.

As he checked the pair of Navy Colts and satisfied himself they were in full working order, he
sucked in the smoke of his cigar as if it alone were
capable of nourishing him.

Pushing the long, blue barrels of his weapons

into his belt so that their grips poked out above his belt buckle, Iron Eyes jabbed his vicious spurs into the horse and allowed it to continue on towards Bonny.

There were those who thought the deadly bounty hunter was an Indian due to his mane of limp black hair, and the fact that his scarred face never seemed capable of growing whiskers upon it like most pale skinned men. There were others who had survived being up close to the tall, thin man who always wore a long weathered dust jacket with deep, bullet-filled pockets, who knew this creature hailed from no known tribe of Indian.

And there were a few who thought Iron Eyes was simply a living ghost that somehow refused to die. Whatever the truth, the cold eyes of the sinister rider had frozen the blood of many a foe, before his deadly-accurate pistols had dispatched them to a more peaceful place.

Perhaps he was an Indian from some unknown tribe which had long ceased to exist. Perhaps he was an avenging spectre from some unholy place who came to claim souls for the Devil himself.

Whatever Iron Eyes was, he was unique. Most thanked the Lord for that small mercy. One Iron Eyes was more than enough for any world.

The night sky and the large moon suited the bounty hunter as he chewed on the end of his cigar. He liked to strike when it was dark; when civilized folks had long retired to their beds and found a dream or two to ease them away from the reality which dominated their waking hours. For the wanted men he sought tended to drink, and womanized during the hours of darkness when decent souls slept. This alone made locating them far easier to a man who was always ready to dispatch his own brand of justice.

As Iron Eyes entered the small one-street town, he noted the couple of horses tied up near the saloon. There were no other horses anywhere else in Bonny. Glancing at the ground from his high perch, his keen eyesight recognized the hoof prints he had followed for so long. Even in the moonlight, his vision was still as honed as it had always been.

Iron Eyes teased the reins of the tired mount and closed in on the saloon, which still harboured people unwilling to leave one day and exchange it for another. The sound of men and females within the saloon drifted out into the street, along with the bad piano playing.

He had never been to Bonny before, but knew it was probably the same as the hundreds of other towns he had ridden into over the years, tracking down the vermin it seemed the law could not find.

Halting the horse at the hitching rail, Iron Eyes sat looking up and down the street until he was satisfied it was empty. It did not take him long to recognize the horse he knew belonged to the outlaw he sought. Finishing his cigar, he tossed it away and readied himself for what he knew lay ahead in the minutes which would follow. Lifting his long, right leg over the neck of his mount, Iron Eyes slid to the ground.

Tying his reins to the wooden upright outside the saloon, the bounty hunter looked across at the outlaw's horse, which still had steam rising from it. Taking twelve paces to the tethered horse of the man he had hunted for so many weeks, Iron Eyes ran a hand along its neck.

It was still wet – wet from the hard ride it had endured as its master had vainly tried to get away from the dogged pursuer, a man who did not know how to give up once he had the scent of his prey in his nostrils.

Iron Eyes rubbed his hand dry on his jacket and began walking back towards the light, which cascaded out from the saloon doorway and reached to the buildings opposite.

He had to be inside, Iron Eyes thought. Drinking and waiting for him to arrive. Maybe the outlaw had convinced himself that he had managed to lose his shadow out there on the massive range of sagebrush. Perhaps he was sitting with his back to the wall with both guns in his hands, waiting for death to walk through the door of the saloon and try and kill before being killed.

Whichever way it panned out, Iron Eyes was ready.

Stepping up on to the boardwalk, Iron Eyes glanced through the window at the half-dozen people who were milling around. Two females of dubious age appeared desperate to make a few dollars from the four men still drinking before they either ran out of money or interest. A bartender seemed more asleep than awake as he leaned on the counter, watching his customers with eyes that had seen it all before so many times. Without pausing, Iron Eyes walked straight into the noisy building and stopped in his tracks.

Within the space of a mere heartbeat, the saloon was silent. Every person within its four walls stared at the gruesome sight before them.

The bounty hunter hovered with his hands above his belt buckle and the two gun grips as his eyes darted around the large room. He knew the face of the man he had chased across the baking-hot range although they had never met. The photographic likeness was on the crumpled Wanted poster in his deep pocket amongst the bullets and cigars. A likeness which was branded into his mind.

Then Iron Eyes saw him.

TWO

The outlaw slowly began to stand up from behind the table as he watched the lethal Iron Eyes standing just inside the doorway of the saloon. Reaching his full height, his keen eyes watched the other five patrons vanish from the vicinity. Even the weary bartender managed to slip out from behind the long bar and disappear into the relative safety of a back room.

In the time it took for the second hand on the wall clock to move less than halfway around the clock face, only two men remained in the saloon. Two very different men.

'Dan Creedy!' The name seemed to drip from the lips of Iron Eyes as he stepped closer. The outlaw's face was now visibly more frightened than the image which was emblazoned on the Wanted poster buried deep in one of Iron Eyes's bullet-filled pockets.

The man walked slowly from behind the round card-table towards the bar. With every step he kept at least one eye fixed on the bounty hunter. Creedy knew that it paid to be cautious of this sort of man.

'Do I know you, stranger? I think I'd have remembered your face if'n we'd ever met before.'

'They call me Iron Eyes,' came the slow, deliberate reply from the thin, emotionless face. 'We ain't ever met but I know who and what you are, Creedy.'

The man seemed to recognize the notorious name and the description of the living ghost who hunted men. He gritted his teeth as he dragged an abandoned whiskey bottle towards him before turning over a small thimble-glass.

'The bounty hunter?'

'The same.' Iron Eyes took another step towards the man, who pulled the cork from the neck of the bottle with his teeth before spitting it into the sawdust at his feet.

'I heard of you,' Creedy said as he poured himself a full measure of the brown liquor.

'I've heard of you too. You're worth $1,000,' Iron Eyes said coldly, 'dead or alive.'

Creedy felt sweat trickling down his face as he rested the bottle down, and then lifted the drink to his lips before pausing to stare at the gruesome sight of the man he knew intended to be his executioner. No wonder the room had cleared at the sight of Iron Eyes, he thought. He had seen a thousand faces, but none like the one staring at him from behind the limp black hair. This was not the face of a man that it was possible to bribe or bluff from his intended course of action. Iron Eyes had only one thing on his mind, and it was the price on Dan Creedy's head.

'Mind if I take me a drink before we get down to business?'

'Nope,' Iron Eyes replied.

Dan Creedy swallowed the whiskey in one go and then placed the glass back down on top of the wet bar. He had killed more than a dozen men with his Colt, but for the first time in his entire life, knew his luck might just be about to run out. After taking several deep breaths, Creedy turned away from the long, wooden counter and faced Iron Eyes.

'I heard stories about you, Iron Eyes,' Creedy said as he pushed his coat over the handle of his gun. 'They say you ain't a living man. They say you're a ghost.'

The bounty hunter nodded.

'It's all true.'

Creedy flexed his fingers and swallowed whilst watching the almost skeletal figure before him. He noted the two gun grips sticking out of the broad belt strapped around Iron Eyes's middle, and wondered how any man could possibly be a quick draw if he had to pull guns from a belt. The more Creedy thought about it, the more convinced he became that no living man could draw weapons from a belt with any speed. It was impossible.

'I guess this is it,' Creedy said as confidence returned to his troubled soul again.

Iron Eyes nodded again.

'Reckon so.'

The ancient clock upon the wall of the saloon suddenly began to chime.

Dan Creedy threw himself to the left and reached for his trusty Colt. His experienced fingers found its grip and drew it from the leather holster tied securely to his thigh. Before the barrel of the pistol had cleared the lip of the holster, his index finger had found the trigger as his thumb cocked its hammer until it locked. Then he squeezed off his first shot.

A cloud of smoke breached the distance between the outlaw and the bounty hunter. It was so dense that both men lost sight of one another. Iron Eyes had pulled both his Navy Colts from his belt and dragged their hammers back before firing. Dropping to the floor, Iron Eyes heard the groaning sound of Creedy as another shot came through the gunsmoke like a bolt of lightning towards him. The bounty hunter felt the heat on his scalp from the bullet as it passed through his hair. He knew if he hadn't dropped on to his knees, the bullet would have gone straight into his middle.

Instinctively, Iron Eyes fired both his pistols again into the cloud which faced him. This time Iron Eyes heard his opponent scream and stagger back into the wooden bar before tottering towards him. Choking gunsmoke filled the distance between the two men as their shots echoed around the wooden building. Then Creedy staggered towards the kneeling bounty hunter, staring with eyes which could no longer see. The gun fell from his fingers and bounced on the floor as the outlaw stopped and hovered.

Iron Eyes stood up again and looked at the four neat bullet holes in the shirt of the unsteady man. Any one of his shots could have killed the outlaw on their own. Together, it was only a matter of how long it would take for Dan Creedy's body to realize that it was dead.

It had not been a long duel. It had ended almost as soon as it had begun.

Slowly, Dan Creedy slumped forward and fell heavily on his face in the stale sawdust. There was a huge gasp as his life seemed to escape like swamp gas from his being. He had been wrong. It was possible to draw guns from your belt if you were Iron Eyes. Creedy had made a mistake. It was to be his last.

21

Walking up to the body, Iron Eyes placed his guns back into his belt and leaned on the bar. It was over and yet he felt nothing. It had been too easy.

As he picked up the whiskey bottle and raised it to his lips he noticed spots of blood dripping on to his hand. Looking up into the cracked, dirty mirror behind the bar, he saw the wound on his scalp. There was a parting in his long, matted mane which had never been there before.

One of Dan Creedy's shots had dug out a chunk of his scalp as it passed over him. Blood was running freely down his face before he managed to finish the contents of the liquor bottle. It was cheap, rotgut whiskey which had probably been made in a tin bathtub out back, but Iron Eyes did not care. Liquor had never managed to make him drunk, however much of it he consumed. Even the most expensive brands had no effect on his pitifully lean frame.

Yet Iron Eyes was confused. He was bleeding badly, but there was no pain from the ugly wound. It did not even sting. It just bled.

Touching his scalp with his long fingers, Iron Eyes found the deep wound in his straggly hair. Dan Creedy's final shot had only been an inch too high, he thought.

Iron Eyes stared at the sticky red blood on the tips of his fingers and paused. Could Creedy have

22

been right when he called the bounty hunter a ghost? Ghosts were already dead and that meant they could not feel pain. But he was bleeding like a stuck pig.

Did ghosts bleed? Why was there no pain? Something just did not add up.

As he turned to face the corpse, he suddenly felt giddy. It was a strange feeling which made him rest his lean frame against the wooden bar. Blood ran down the strands of hair before his eyes and dripped. It was a continuous flow of crimson droplets which meant the wound was probably far worse than he had first thought. Yet it still did not hurt.

Why didn't it hurt? Iron Eyes was troubled by this strange truth. His head was filled with a fog that seemed reluctant to clear.

Stepping away from the bar, Iron Eyes stood over the body of Dan Creedy and looked down at it for several seconds. He waited until his thoughts became sharp again. There was something strange about the outlaw that Iron Eyes had noticed just before they had drawn their guns and fired. Dan Creedy had seemed to be totally unafraid. Not at first when Iron Eyes had entered the saloon, but a split second before they had gone for their weapons.

Why was the outlaw unafraid? Did he know something which Iron Eyes had yet to learn?

23

Iron Eyes leaned over, grabbed the collar of his prize and then lifted it off the ground and hauled it out into the deserted street. Looking around the wooden structures he finally saw the sheriff's office.

Above the locked office door, Iron Eyes spied a small window and a dim light behind its lace drape. Dragging the body of his prey across the street towards the office, Iron Eyes felt his long, bony legs buckling for a moment. Somehow he managed to continue until his mule-ear boots found the opposite boardwalk and mounted it. Then he released his grip and dropped the lifeless body at his feet.

Resting his bleeding head against the wall, he began hitting the door with a clenched fist.

Iron Eyes wanted his reward money. He also wanted to know where the nearest doctor was. As his fist struck the door for the tenth time, he saw a man through its glass pane, carrying a candle inside the building, walking hurriedly towards him.

As the man in the white nightgown slid the bolt across on the door, Iron Eyes felt his legs buckle again.

This time, as the door was opened, he was unable to prevent himself from falling at the man's naked feet.

THREE

Iron Eyes had stubbornly refused to lie down on the leather couch within the back room of the doctor's office. Even when only half-conscious, he had refused to submit to the demands of either the sheriff or the doctor. The bounty hunter had sat bolt upright on a hardback chair since a half-dressed sheriff had helped him from the board-walk outside his front door, along to the dimly illuminated building.

There was a silence about Iron Eyes which kept both the lawman and the physician on their toes as his scalp was carefully stitched back together. Neither man had heard him say anything during the long operation.

It was an unnerving sight to see anyone covered in so much of their own blood, but on Iron Eyes, it seemed an even worse apparition. Both the doctor and the sheriff might have thought he

25

was dead if it had not been for the cold, staring grey eyes which continually watched them.

Iron Eyes stared occasionally at the floor during the procedure, and kept looking at the pools of blood which covered it. It was his blood. He also wondered why he could not feel the long needle as it was forced through the skin on his scalp, dragging it back together.

For two hours the sweating physician had toiled over the head of Iron Eyes until he finally satisfied himself that he had stemmed the flow of blood.

The doctor stepped backwards and studied his handiwork before picking up a pair of long-bladed scissors and trimming the ends of the catgut.

'This stitching will have to be removed in about a week or so, otherwise it will go septic, stranger,' the doctor informed his silent patient.

Iron Eyes glanced up at the elderly doctor.

'How do I get this fishing line out of my head, doc?'

The doctor shrugged as he dropped the scissors into the blood-soaked kidney dish which matched his once-white nightgown.

'It will have to be removed by a doctor, my boy.'

'In my line of work, I don't run into your sort very often.' Iron Eyes touched the wound again. 'I wanna know how I can remove it myself.'

The doctor cleared his throat as the sheriff walked around the seated man.

'Cut the stitches at both ends and then carefully slide it out,' the medical man replied. 'If you do it wrong, it'll hurt really bad. I advise you try and get a doctor to do it.'

Iron Eyes nodded. 'I'll try and find a doctor to do it.'

'What's eating at you, son?' The doctor could see the face of the seated man seemed troubled by something. Whatever it was, it had to be important, he thought.

'I can't feel nothing, doc,' Iron Eyes said bluntly to the two men before him as he tapped the wound with his fingers. 'The whole top of my head is dead. It has been since Dan Creedy parted my scalp with his last shot.'

The sheriff rubbed his chin and watched the concerned doctor stepping closer to the seated stranger. The elderly physician stepped to the back of his patient and then picked up the scissors again.

'I'm going to touch your scalp, son. Tell me when I do so.'

Iron Eyes grunted. 'OK, doc. See if you can figure it out.'

The doctor lifted the scissors and touched the neat stitches carefully with its closed blades. There was no reaction from Iron Eyes as he moved the blade along the entire length of the grotesque wound.

27

'When you gonna start, old man?' Iron Eyes asked.

'I already started and finished, son,' the doctor said as he dropped the metal scissors into the dish once again, and moved around to look straight at the face hiding behind the limp, blood-stained mane of hair.

'Well? What does it mean?' Iron Eyes rose to his feet and felt his legs buckle again before he managed to regain his balance.

'It could be that the bullet ripped the nerves in your scalp to shreds, stranger,' the doctor said while watching the tall man moving around his room.

'Will it return to normal?' Iron Eyes asked as he glanced across at the two men, who were watching him the way men watch animals in circus cages.

'It might be temporary and then again it could be permanent.'

The bounty hunter still felt giddy as he placed his hands on the back of the wooden chair and rested.

'How come I feel like there's a fog inside my skull?'

'That might be due to the fact you've lost an awful lot of blood, son,' the doctor answered.

'Will this be temporary?'

The doctor shrugged.

'Hopefully. I suggest you eat as much steak as possible over the next week to try and replace the blood you've lost.'

'Steak.' Iron Eyes repeated the word as he handed over a fistful of silver dollars to the medical man.

The sheriff stepped closer to the strange bounty hunter.

'I wired the authorities for your reward money just after I brung you to the doc's, mister. Who exactly are you, anyways?'

'They call me Iron Eyes, Sheriff.'

Suddenly the two men seemed alarmed. It was obvious to the bounty hunter that they had heard of him and his reputation frightened them.

'It will probably take until around noon before I get permission to pay you the bounty, Iron Eyes,' the sheriff said dryly as he felt the spittle in his mouth evaporating. 'Might even take longer.'

'That'll be fine, Sheriff.' Iron Eyes glanced at the law officer who was still wearing his nightshirt.

The sheriff cleared his throat.

'How much do you know about the late Dan Creedy, Iron Eyes?'

'Only his value.'

The doctor moved towards both men and touched the arm of the lawman.

'What are you getting at, Sheriff?'

'Dan Creedy has three brothers and by what

29

I've heard, they rode together,' the sheriff mumbled. 'I figure they'll be a tad upset when they hear the news. They'll hunt you down and get their vengeance, Iron Eyes.'

'They can try.' Iron Eyes almost smiled.

'You mean that they might be close at hand?' the doctor asked his troubled friend. 'They might swoop down into Bonny and shoot up the town trying to find out who killed their brother?'

'Yeah, they might have arranged to meet up in Bonny. They ain't gonna like finding Dan dead.' The lawman knew more about the Creedys than he was either able or willing to admit.

Iron Eyes stood upright and then began walking to the door of the dimly-lit office. Resting a hand on the door handle, he paused and looked back at the pair of elderly men. They had shown him kindness and he found it confusing.

'Quit fretting, boys. As soon as I get my reward money, I'll ride out of this damn town. If'n them Creedys want to trail me, let them. I'll be waiting to collect their rewards too.'

'Ain't you even a little bit scared of Dan's brothers, boy?' the sheriff asked as Iron Eyes turned the handle and opened the door. 'I heard tell that they're mighty mean.'

'Meaner than me?' Iron Eyes raised an eyebrow.

'Maybe,' the sheriff gulped.

'There ain't no such critter, Sheriff.'

Watching Iron Eyes striding out into the dark street, both men seemed unable to take their eyes from him as he headed back in the direction of the saloon. Both men were aware that this was no ordinary stranger they had within the boundaries of Bonny. This was Iron Eyes and he had killed Dan Creedy for the price on his head.

How long would it take for the Creedy brothers to arrive?

FOUR

Iron Eyes had somehow stayed awake for what remained of the blood-soaked night. Primed with an inch-thick steak and two bottles of whiskey, the bounty hunter seemed either unwilling or uninterested in finding a place to sleep until dawn. He had done what he had set out to do and killed Dan Creedy, but it had been a close call. Creedy had not wanted to die and looked as if he truly believed he could defeat Iron Eyes. The thought troubled the skeletal figure as he stared into his glass, because for the first time in all his years of hunting down outlaws, he had been seriously wounded.

The saloon had remained open for the solitary customer, who sat at a table only a few feet away from the blood-stained sawdust which bore evidence to his last conquest. The bartender snored in an easy chair as Iron Eyes continued to pour one measure after another of the amber liquid into his glass.

Iron Eyes cast his hollow bullet-coloured pupils around the silent saloon, and wondered how much more blood he could have afforded to lose before he would have joined Dan Creedy in the very bowels of Lucifer's eternal flames. Iron Eyes had been wounded many times before but had never bled like that. He stared at the pool of red sawdust near the bar and the trail which led out of the saloon.

As the sun finally rose far off in the prairie and light washed over the small township of Bonny, Iron Eyes continued drinking his whiskey. Whatever this new day had in store for him, he would face it with the same contempt he had faced all of the others.

He had eaten the steak meal as advised by the elderly doctor but felt no better. How long did it take for blood to be made in a body such as his anyway? Iron Eyes had tried to understand the old physician's words but, to him, it did not make any sense. How could eating grub make blood? Maybe it was because steak was usually filled with blood and the doctor meant that as long as he somehow consumed the red liquid, it would fill his empty veins.

Iron Eyes rubbed his face angrily. As the morning light entered the saloon, he noticed the dried blood which stained the shoulders of his coat. The browning patches stretched down his sleeves and covered most of his clothing.

Dan Creedy's last shot would have killed most men, but Iron Eyes was not like other men. Perhaps the outlaw's words had been true and he was already dead. Looking at the evidence of how much blood he had lost, the bounty hunter wondered if there could possibly be any left.

The whiskey had gone down his throat better than the tough steak. It always went down better. If the doctor had said that drinking vast volumes of rotgut liquor made blood, Iron Eyes could have seen the sense in it. At least both were liquid.

He touched the stitches and wondered again why his scalp was still totally numb. Would it matter if it stayed that way? It might even be an advantage in the future should anyone break a chair over his skull.

The giddiness had not troubled him since he had left the doctor's house. Maybe it had only happened because his head had been split open and once it was sewn back together, it was a thing of the past.

Iron Eyes liked that idea. He swallowed another glass of the whiskey and stared down again at the sawdust before him. Dan Creedy's body had been removed by someone before he had returned to the saloon. He knew that the sheriff

must have awoken the town undertaker when he
had wired off for permission to pay the bounty
money. So much blood had been spilled on to the
sawdust, and most of it had been his own.

He could still see the outline in the sawdust
where Creedy's lifeless body had lain.

The sound of a rooster echoed off the buildings
around the silent saloon. Iron Eyes pushed the
plate away from him and rose to his feet. He
carried the whiskey bottle in his hand and
replaced its cork into the black glass neck before
dropping it into one of his deep pockets.

The town was still asleep as he walked out on
to the boardwalk and looked at his pitiful horse. It
was in a sorrowful state but Iron Eyes had never
cared for horses. To him, they were simply things
which he rode until they dropped, and then he
simply acquired a replacement.

Finding one of his long, black cigars amid the
countless bullets in his other coat pocket, Iron
Eyes placed it between his sharp teeth and then
found a box of matches in his shirt pocket.

The heat was already rising off everything the
blazing morning sun touched as the bounty
hunter strode across the street in the direction of
the sound coming from the noisy rooster.

Rounding the corner, Iron Eyes spied a small
fenced-off garden filled with a score of hens peck-
ing at the ground, and the long-necked colourful

cock-bird standing upon the henhouse. Iron Eyes walked up to the fence and lit his cigar.

It had been a long while since he had been so close to such a domestic creature, and the scene that faced him seemed strange. He did not like it.

The rooster continued crowing at the rising sun as smoke drifted from Iron Eyes's mouth. Faster than the blink of an eye, he drew one of his Navy Colts from his belt, cocked its hammer and fired a single shot.

As the head of the rooster went in a different direction to that of its body, the bounty hunter turned and began walking back towards the saloon.

'That'll teach him.' He smiled.

They were a gruesome-looking bunch by anyone's yardstick. The trio of dust-caked riders attracted the attention of every eye along the main street of the sprawling town of Tequila Flats as they rode into its heart. Set a mere twenty miles south of the remote Bonny, Tequila Flats was everything the smaller town was not and would never be.

It had wealth, and it showed.

Dawn had only just broken a mere twenty minutes earlier, but the streets were teeming with more people than the three riders had seen in over a month of riding. Too many people, they thought. Too many curious people.

It had not been part of their original plan to enter the boundaries of such a prosperous town because they knew, where there was money, there were usually far too many law officers ready and willing to protect it. Tequila Flats overflowed with well-armed deputies who knew how to use their weaponry and prayed for any excuse to prove themselves to their sheriff.

The Creedy brothers eased their mounts through the busy streets until they located the large livery stables at the very heart of the town. They knew coming here was risky, but they also knew something was wrong, otherwise they would have already met up with their brother, Dan. There had to be a good reason for his not joining his brothers and they had to try and find out what.

Entering Tequila Flats might furnish the answers. It might also furnish them with coffins if just one of the law officers recognized their dust-covered faces and found the Wanted posters they matched.

Bob Creedy was a man of greying appearance who seemed far older than his twenty-eight years. He dismounted first outside the impressive livery stable, as his brothers carefully looked back at the curious town residents before getting off their saddles.

Treat Creedy was very similar in looks yet had

colour in his hair and skin. He was less than a year younger than Bob, but looked at least ten years Bob's junior. He held on to his reins and watched the faces that observed them with a sharpness that he had honed to a fine art, for he was the gang's lookout.

The youngest of the Creedys was called Frankie, and was far shorter than any of his brothers. He looked little more than a boy, but in truth was nearly twenty-four years of age. He had killed a man for each of his years with the pair of deadly Remingtons he wore hidden beneath his trail coat. Frankie Creedy was by far the most lethal of any of them, yet looked the epitome of sweetness and light.

The brothers handed the reins of their mounts over to the stable man, and then rested on the edge of a water trough as they pondered the large, busy town around them.

So many people, so many eyes. Eyes which were trained only on them.

They had not wanted to ride into this town because they knew only too well of its reputation. This was a town that did not tolerate scum. It said so on a crudely-painted sign just before the larger sign bearing the name of the town, on the edge of Tequila Flats.

'I reckon we ought to stay away from the banks,' Bob Creedy said as he placed his pipe between his teeth and struck a match along the side of his gun grip. 'I figure these varmints will figure we are here to rob one of them.'

'Ain't gonna be easy,' Treat sighed.

'Yeah, this whole town is filled with banks,' Frankie noted as he rubbed the trail dust from his deceptively youthful features.

'Never seen so many banks.' Treat raised an eyebrow as he looked at Bob, who was sucking the flame of his match into his pipe bowl. 'Kinda tempting.'

'Forget it. Treat. We ain't here to rob no banks,' the older Creedy snapped as he tossed his match away. 'It would be suicide in this town.'

'Then how come we came here?'

'To rest our horses and get us some grub and provisions.' Bob puffed on his pipe.

'And?' Treat pressed.

'And to try and find out why Dan didn't meet us at Powder River like we arranged.' Bob Creedy stood up again and gripped the pipe stem in his teeth as he studied the people who were milling around in the busy street.

'What can we find out here?' Frankie asked as he cupped water in his hands and splashed it over his face.

'They got themselves a telegraph office here and they also got a newspaper office, boys.' Bob sucked in smoke and allowed it to filter through his teeth as he spoke.

'So?' Treat stood.

'How else do we find if anything's happened to Dan?' Bob replied as he carefully checked his guns with his back to the crowd.

Frankie rubbed his face dry on his bandanna as he eased himself up beside his brothers. He appeared even younger with the dirt washed off his face. Almost childlike. It was a deadly illusion.

'You reckon Dan might be dead?'

'Yep. I figure only death would stop Dan from meeting up with us, boys,' Bob Creedy interrupted as he began walking slowly back towards the main street and the crowds of neatly-dressed people who still seemed unable to take their eyes off them. 'Come on. We ain't gonna get nothing done sitting outside a stable.'

'I don't like the way these bastards are eyeing us, Bob,' the sweating Frankie snarled from beneath his youthful features. 'I reckon we ought to get our carbines, just in case.'

Bob glanced at the youngster.

'We have to look like ordinary folks just passing through, Frankie. If we are carrying our Winchesters, I figure it'll take five minutes before we are surrounded by every damn lawman in this town.'

'What if we run into the sheriff or his deputies?' Treat asked.

'We'll have to try and talk our way out of trouble,' Bob said firmly.

'What if they ain't the talkative kind?'

'We'll have to try and shoot our way back to the horses,' Bob sighed as they drew closer to the main street once more. 'That's our last resort. I don't want no shooting unless there ain't no option.'

'I knew this was a dumb thing to do, riding into this blasted place.' Treat shook his head as he walked beside his brothers.

'Just keep smiling, Treat,' Bob Creedy advised as he tipped his dusty Stetson to passing women carrying their baskets. 'A smile can confuse even the smartest of folks.'

The three brothers moved cautiously. They knew it was only a matter of time before one or more of this town's numerous deputies bumped into them. They had to try and act like normal folks until they discovered the information they sought.

It was not going to be easy. None of the three men could remember the last time they had actually been normal folks without a price on their heads. If they were to survive in Tequila Flats long enough to learn about their brother's fate, they had to try and not look like the deadly thieves and killers they really were.

It would not be easy, for with every step the

41

three Creedy brothers took as they walked deeper into the streets of Tequila Flats, the Devil seemed to ring out a tune of warning on their razor-sharp spurs.

FIVE

There were ten heavily-laden wagons filled with more than sixty gold miners pulled by the same amount of oxen slowly heading towards the tall hills. Flanked by nearly a hundred troopers, this was no ordinary expedition that was entering the reservation of the Southern Cheyenne, but something far more ominous.

This was an army of scavengers. Men who did nothing except ravage nature for the yellow nuggets which were prized above all things, including life itself. Men willing and able to destroy entire mountains just to take the golden ore from beneath its soil. Men who, for some reason, were being protected by the US Cavalry.

The straight-backed officer at the head of the cavalry troop and swollen wagons had never knowingly disobeyed an order in his entire career. A career which stretched back twenty years to the

West Point Military Academy, yet for the first time in that illustrious career he knew that he was aiding and abetting something which was fundamentally wrong. Entering the land of the peaceful Cheyenne did not sit well with the man who had always prided himself on doing the right thing.

Major Thomas Roberts had not spoken more than a dozen words since he had left Fort Bruce a week earlier. He had done his talking to try and stop this violation but all his pleading had come to nothing. It was as if everything he held dear – about morality and how the white men should not continue to take advantage of the Indians – fell on ears either unable or unwilling to listen. Roberts had reluctantly accepted the duty forced upon him with a heavy heart.

Yet with every passing mile he knew this was wrong. Not just morally but legally.

Every objection Major Roberts had given his superiors within the tall, wooden walls of the prairie fortress, had been totally ignored. He had tried to reason with them, but there was something else behind the orders he was not privy to. Now he knew that if anyone were to head this band of ruthless miners, it had to be him. Major Roberts realized that he was probably the only chance the Cheyenne had of not being lured into something they were incapable of winning.

As the elegant horseman steered his grey

charger deeper and deeper into the land which only five years earlier had been given to the Cheyenne, supposedly for eternity, he glanced at the tree-covered hills which rose to both sides and knew there might be eyes behind every tree-trunk, watching them.

A hundred questions had constantly filled Roberts's mind since he had first been given his orders to escort the gold miners into the land where thousands of Cheyenne lived peacefully. What could have possessed Colonel Harker to give permission to the mining company? Why would he risk starting another Indian war?

Major Roberts knew he might never truly find the answers he sought because there was more behind this than met the eye. During the years he had served in the cavalry out west, he had witnessed one broken treaty after another – seen entire tribes of Indians obliterated from the face of the prairies simply because they were standing in the way of progress.

The East required expansion to settle the hostile lands so it had a market for the goods being manufactured in its factories. Guns and ploughs were being made by the million, and the west provided customers.

The Indians of the plains required nothing but the land itself, and stood in the way of the plans which had been created to join the west coast with the eastern one. They had to be removed by any means possible.

As Major Roberts gripped the reins of his grey mount firmly in his white gauntlets, he knew that the Cheyenne had been given land that was later discovered to be rich in gold. This meant that they too were to be sacrificed like the countless other tribes he had seen driven to extinction. The other plains Indians had simply occupied land which the powers back East wanted to release to settlers as the American Nation forged further and further West. But a land filled with gold was even more tempting.

Major Roberts glanced back at his troopers and the wagons behind him before returning his attention to the tall grassland ahead. He was party to an outrage and yet felt he could do nothing except follow his orders.

Roberts knew that if the Cheyenne attacked, as was their right, he would have to defend the miners. The papers in Washington would say that the hostile savaged has attacked the US Cavalry and broken the peace treaty. There would be nobody to tell the truth and defend the Cheyenne.

Roberts reined in his mount and stopped the caravan of invaders. Sitting on his high saddle he pulled out his binoculars and searched the hills for signs that they might have already been noticed. There were none.

He gave a sigh of relief as he dismounted. There was still enough time to turn around and withdraw from this place, he thought, as he watched miners clambering from their wagons and troopers from their horses. Still enough time to get out of this reservation and head back to Fort Bruce.

As he slid the binoculars back into his saddlebags, Sergeant John Walker rode up beside him. Walker was a big man with a smiling face that belied his courage.

Climbing off his horse, the well-built sergeant strode to the side of his superior and removed his battered white hat.

'What we stopped here for, sir?'

Roberts bit his lip.

'I'm not venturing any further today, Walker.'

'But it ain't even noon yet,' Sergeant Walker said staring at the low sun which had many hours to go before reaching directly over their heads.

'Are you in a hurry, John?' Major Roberts stared into the face of the big man.

Walker rubbed the sweat off his brow and gazed along the valley ahead of them at the countless tree-covered mountainous peaks.

'I reckon I understand, sir.'

'Good. I'm in no hurry to reach our destination because once we do, I think we'll have a fight on our hands.' Roberts gave the miners a sly look. He had nothing but contempt for the rough, evil-smelling men he was escorting.

'Where do you figure the Cheyenne camp is?' Walker asked.

Major Thomas Roberts did not reply, but stared down the long valley of lush swaying grass. Somewhere down there in the heart of this forbidden land, at least five thousand unsuspecting Cheyenne were going about their daily rituals.

How long would it be before they spotted them?

SIX

Bob Creedy sucked on his pipe and watched the street from within the relative safety of the quiet cafe as his brothers ate. He was nervous and, even behind the veil of smoke which cascaded from his mouth, looked so.

'Ease up, Bob,' Frankie Creedy said as he chewed the last of his breakfast before washing it down his throat with a mouthful of black coffee.

'The boy's right, Bob. Take it easy,' Treat Creedy said as he rubbed his mouth along the back of his sleeve before rising to his feet.

Bob Creedy said nothing as he puffed frantically on the stem of his hot pipe. He knew this was not a place where their sort could relax for even an instant. Tequila Flats was dangerous.

The small, aged waitress stood watching her three customers with a terror she had never felt before. The woman knew that these men were unlike any she had served before in the small cafe. Yet they had done nothing which gave her reason to do anything except continue refilling their cups with the strong black beverage.

Treat Creedy walked around the small table and moved to the side of his older brother. He knew Bob was the one member of his family who worried. Maybe that was why he looked so drained of colour.

'You eat and I'll watch out for trouble, Bob.'

Bob Creedy dragged the pipe from his lips and then glanced at the face of his brother.

'I ain't hungry. I got me a knot in my guts.'

'Then have some coffee for heaven's sake,' Treat urged.

Bob nodded reluctantly.

'OK. Bring me a cup.'

As Frankie began to get up from the table with the coffee pot in his hand, he noticed the faces of his two brothers suddenly alter as they spotted something out in the busy street.

'What is it? What ya seen?' Frankie asked as he rushed to the side of the two taller men.

'Trouble, I reckon,' Bob Creedy muttered as he stuffed the pipe into his pocket and flicked the safety loops off his pistols.

Treat Creedy gave the interior of the cafe a fast inspection before returning his attention to the pair of men walking down the boardwalk in their direction. They were tall, well-fed men and both wore gleaming tin stars on their shirts.

'The law!'

'We'll have to shoot our way back to the horses,' Frankie whispered into the ear of Bob.

Bob Creedy rubbed his face with his fingers as his brain raced.

'Nope. We ain't gonna do nothing dumb. We are going to bluff our way out of this pickle.'

Treat felt his mouth drying as the two men drew closer to the cafe. They were flanked by dozens of the town's residents – mostly women, all talking continuously to the law officers.

'I figure them folks went and told them deputies of our arrival, boys,' Bob Creedy said quietly as he stared out through the clean window panes at the Winchester-toting pair of deputies.

'This looks bad,' Treat panted heavily as he peered over his older brother's shoulder.

'Stop fretting,' Bob ordered. 'Let me do all the talking and we'll get out of this without a scratch.'

'Are you sure?' Frankie gulped.

Bob Creedy inhaled deeply and then tossed a couple of silver dollars on to the top of the table and touched his hat brim at the waitress. Then he led his two younger brothers out into the street and smiled at the approaching crowd.

The two deputies stopped in their tracks. The crowd stopped several paces behind them. It was as if they had never seen three men quite so trail-weary in appearance as the Creedy brothers.

'Didn't you boys see the sign outside town?' one of the deputies asked as he clutched his carbine across his belly.

'We seen it, deputy.' Bob Creedy forced the widest smile he had ever mustered and stepped one place closer to the two nervous lawmen.

'We don't cotton to scum in Tequila Flats,' the second deputy added.

Bob Creedy nodded.

'Neither do we. That's why we're here. Me and the boys are bounty hunters on the trail of a mighty bad piece of work called Dan Creedy.'

'Bounty hunters?' The two law officers seemed to repeat the word at exactly the same time.

'Sorry we look a tad dirty, but it has been a long haul getting to this place. We ain't had no time to wash up and put on our Sunday best,' Bob Creedy continued to add to his story.

'What's you name?' one of the men asked.

'I'm Bob Custer and this is Joe and Jim Smith.' Bob somehow managed to smile as the curious eyes kept burning into them.

'How come you came to Tequila Flats?' The question seemed to come from the crowd behind the two deputies.

'We lost the trail of this Creedy character a couple of days back. I figured it would make sense to come here and check out the newspapers and send a few wires,' Bob retorted quickly.

'That's damn smart,' the first deputy grinned. 'It sure pays to be a real professional and know all them kinda tricks. You send a few wires to other towns and you can find out where this Creedy bastard is.'

'You boys sure know your business, OK,' the second deputy agreed.

SEVEN

There was no mistaking the image that tore across what remained of the prairie towards the tree-covered hills and distant mountains. The horse was new, paid for out of the $1,000 reward money, but the rider was unmistakable.

No one who had ever seen this ghost-like rider could or would ever mistake him for any other. With his black hair whipping the back of his blood-stained long coat, like the flapping wings of a vulture, Iron Eyes drove mercilessly on and on.

There was no longer anything in Bonny for the bounty hunter now that he had the silver and gold coins of his latest slaying filling the saddle-bags behind his saddle cantle. Iron Eyes could have remained for another few days and allowed his severe head injuries to heal, but something had forced him to discard the old horse and hit the trail with a new one.

Now Iron Eyes had to find another face which matched one on the crumpled posters in his deep pockets. Yet for all his riding, he was not chasing anyone at all. There was something else forcing him furiously onward. Something he neither knew or understood. He was like a moth being lured against its will, into the light of a naked flame.

Heading towards the tall trees, Iron Eyes knew he would at least be able to find game, and hone some of his original hunting skills in the forests which rose over the hills and into the mountains.

It had been a long time since Iron Eyes had hunted simply for food rather than money; a time when he had tracked and trapped animals for their meat and their pelts to feed and clothe himself. The trees ahead of his charging horse beckoned to him, like the call of old when he was younger and less tarnished by the ways of civilization.

Iron Eyes drove his spurs into the flesh of his new mount and raced across the sagebrush-covered plain feverishly. It was as if he were being dragged back to a place where he had left his innocence. A place so far back in his bloody past that he could no longer remember when or where it had been. All he knew for certain was that it had been another Iron Eyes who had existed then. A man who had not yet discovered how easy it was to kill humans for the price others placed upon their heads.

These, however, were new hills and mountains. Iron Eyes had never been here before and wondered what lay within the dark forests that faced him across the heat-haze of the dusty, dry range. Whatever lay within the depths of the cool forest would be something he had not experienced since embarking on his present occupation.

Iron Eyes felt the heart burning the side of his scarred face as he dragged his reins up and brought the exhausted horse to a sudden halt. Pulling the fresh whiskey bottle out of his saddlebags behind him, he sat staring at the mighty unknown land before him.

Where was this place?

Was it Texas or somewhere else?

Did it even have a name?

So many thoughts filled his mind as the agonizing pain tore through his head like a lightning bolt once more.

Iron Eyes felt strange as he gulped at the neck of the whiskey bottle and then replaced its cork. His head was filled with a throbbing pain which simply would not quit. Iron Eyes had tried to outride the agony, but it was impossible. It was like trying to run away from your own soul.

The painful confusion which had overwhelmed him after he had been wounded had returned with a vengeance.

Sliding the bottle back into his saddlebags and then lowering the leather flap back into place, Iron Eyes dug his spurs back into the horse and rode on.

The forest was drawing him to its bosom like the mother he had never known. He felt that in the cool shade of the tall pines he just might discover who or what he really was. He knew that he could not be a ghost as many claimed, because even he knew that ghosts felt no pain. The blinding explosions which filled his skull proved one thing: he was not yet dead.

Iron Eyes had to reach the alluring forest and try and find a way to clear his mind of the confusion and pain which tortured him. There had been so many battles and so many injuries during his life, and yet none as bad as this one. As the horse gathered speed and began tearing across the dry dusty ground again, Iron Eyes gritted his teeth. He had to try and reach this new place, and perhaps find a peace he had long forgotten actually existed.

As he drove the pitiful horse on, Iron Eyes began to feel giddy again. Gripping the reins tightly with both his skeletal hands, he knew there was no reason to be heading on his present course, yet he continued.

Iron Eyes rode on.

EIGHT

It was a grim-faced Bob Creedy that walked towards his brothers from the telegraph office flanked by the pair of more-than-helpful deputies. They had escorted the oldest Creedy to the newspaper office and then on to the telegraph office, searching for news of Dan. It was obvious by Bob's pained expression, which was carved into his rugged features, that his worst fears had been confirmed.

Dan was dead.

Treat Creedy was leaning on a wooden upright next to his younger brother who had perched his butt on a rickety hitching pole.

'Something's wrong by the look on old Bob's face,' Treat said as he tapped his brother's shoulder and pointed at the three approaching men.

Frankie Creedy stood up from off the corner of the hitching pole and moved towards his eldest brother, as Treat looked at the ground and shook his head knowingly.

'Dan is dead,' Bob mumbled.

'Dead? How?' Frankie licked his cracked lips as he watched the faces of the smiling deputies to either side of his mourning brother. 'Explain.'

'Iron Eyes!' Bob Creedy spat out the name as if it were poison. 'He gunned down Dan in a small town called Bonny and claimed the reward. It's all over the wires.'

'What the hell was Dan doing there?' Frankie asked as he tried to take in the fact that their most able sibling was now dead. It seemed impossible to fathom how anyone could get the better of Dan.

'I figure Iron Eyes chased him there and then gunned him down,' Bob said, trying to accept that Dan could have been killed by the infamous bounty hunter. To him and the rest of the Creedy brothers, Dan had been invincible. Yet he was dead. 'Maybe he was back shot.'

Frankie nodded violently.

'That must be it. Even Iron Eyes could not have gotten the better of Dan in a fair fight.'

'Who is this Iron Eyes varmint, boys?' one of the deputies asked.

'He's a bounty hunter,' Treat responded as he kicked at the dusty ground angrily.

'Like you boys,' the other deputy said.

Bob Creedy glanced up.

'Nope. Not like us, son. Iron Eyes ain't nothing like us.'

The faces of the law officers went blank as the eldest Creedy walked away from the small group and headed towards a saloon clenching his fists.

'What's wrong with him?' one of them asked out loud.

Treat Creedy patted the two men on the shoulders as he steered Frankie away from them.

'Bob don't like us losing bounty money to someone like Iron Eyes, deputies.'

'Who is this Iron Eyes critter?' one of the lawmen asked again as the dust-caked men began to trail their brother in the direction of the saloon.

'They say that he's a dead man,' Treat Cassidy answered over his shoulder. 'They also say he can't be killed because he ain't alive like normal folks.'

'That don't make no sense,' the deputy called out.

'How can a living man be dead?' the other chipped in.

'Iron Eyes ain't like other men,' Treat Creedy sighed heavily as he mounted the boardwalk with his brother in tow.

'He'll be dead when I catch up with the bastard,' Frankie snarled as he was herded into the saloon by the taller Treat.

'Them boys sure take their job seriously,' one of the deputies said to the other as they both turned away.

The afternoon sun was blistering in its intensity as it hovered overhead. The hundred cavalry troopers had made camp and the miners' wagons had been circled under the instructions of the wary army officer.

It was quiet in the centre of the lush valley, yet none of the men who went about their duties seemed capable of relaxing. The miners were consoling themselves with the barrels of liquor they had brought along on their journey, but the soldiers knew this was no place to soak one's brains in whiskey. This place required each and every man to remain alert, for somewhere out there beyond the edge of the valley, thousands of Cheyenne were going about their daily business, unaware their land had been invaded. Major Roberts knew that situation could change with his next heartbeat.

At any moment a hunting party might spot the ten white canvas-topped wagons and more than a hundred souls camped deep inside the Southern Cheyenne reservation boundaries. It would not take long for a young warrior to ride his pony back to the main Indian settlement and inform their elders and chiefs.

Only the Lord above them had any idea of what would then happen.

Major Thomas Roberts knew they were all living on borrowed time, and yet still found himself unable to think of a way out of this sordid situation without disobeying orders and finding himself court-martialled.

What ought he do? The question burned into his soul like a cowboy's red-hot branding iron. He had not eaten or taken anything to drink in the four or five hours since he had halted the caravan of gold miners. His innards were twisted with worry as he continually walked around the makeshift parameter of the camp. He had fought the Southern Cheyenne once before and knew they were a noble adversary, but he did not wish to repeat the action.

His attention was continually drawn to the faces of his young troopers who had no idea of the danger that loomed over this perilous mission. On the whole, they were innocent and untested in battle, and did not deserve to be baptized by facing the wrath of the Cheyenne.

Even if every one of his troop had been a seasoned veteran, Roberts doubted if they would last more than an hour against the thousands of Cheyenne braves upon the reservation.

Unfortunately, his men were not seasoned veterans.

Major Roberts entered the encircled wagons and sought out the one man he knew was the unofficial leader of the gold miners. As the cavalry officer approached the large campfire where men were still eating and drinking, Roberts spotted the unmistakable figure of Bull Fergis.

Fergis was no more than five feet in height but was almost as wide. He seemed to have never shaved or had his hair cut, and had an accent that defied anyone from knowing where it had originated. As the major strode towards him, he marched up to the elegant figure and began ranting.

'If'n I didn't know better, I'd reckon you was scared of taking me and my men to the spot you was told to, Major,' Fergis shouted up at the officer. 'I figure we ought to be another five miles down this valley where the big mountain lies.'

Roberts inhaled deeply before speaking.

'I'm scared all right, Mr Fergis. Scared of us all being surrounded by thousands of irate Cheyenne. You are totally correct about us being on the wrong site, but this is as close as I want to go.'

Bull Fergis rubbed his beard. He was taken aback by the man's frank admission.

'What? You admit it?'

'Exactly. I'm scared. Scared of taking all our men to their deaths.' Major Roberts began to walk

slowly towards the gap between two of the wagons
with the muscular miner at his side. Reaching the
wagon traces, Roberts placed the heel of one of his
boots on the wooden pole that pointed down the
valley. 'There has to be at least five thousand
Cheyenne down there somewhere, Mr Fergis.
Men, women and children. The trouble is, at least
a third of them are men. Young men.'

Bull Fergis seemed shocked.

'Thousands of them, you say?'

'Yes. Thousands of men of an age when fighting
comes as second nature.' Roberts gave the shorter
man a glance before raising his hand and pointing
at the high tree-covered hills that flanked their
small camp. 'For all we know, there could be a
Cheyenne brave behind every tree.'

'Are they armed?'

Roberts nodded. 'Undoubtedly.'

'Hell. Me and the boys weren't told nothing
about no damn Injuns.' Bull Fergis swallowed
hard as a single bead of sweat trickled down from
beneath his hairline and ran over his wrinkled
features.

'What?' Thomas Roberts stared hard at the
miner. 'The mining company did not tell you that
you were being escorted into an Indian Reservation?'

'Nope,' Fergis snapped. 'They kinda forgot that
little gem when they told us about the job. All we

65

were told was that we had to find high grade ore and then ready the site for when the company send in the bigger team. I think I'd remember if'n they'd mentioned Cheyenne. Are they dangerous?'

Roberts rubbed his eyes. 'Only to folks who break the treaty.'

'Like us,' Bull Fergis added.

Major Roberts felt the hair of his neck rising as a cold shudder raced through him. These miners had been duped into getting themselves slaughtered, in order that some greater power might then send in a larger force to seek revenge and proclaim the treaty null and void. These miners were meant to die, as was he and his troopers. Then the Cheyenne would be destroyed and this land would become nothing more than a very prosperous gold mine from one end to the other.

'What'll we do, Major?' Bull Fergis asked.

Major Thomas Roberts said nothing. He was desperately trying to think of a solution to their problem. The trouble was, he was no politician. He had always been an honest man.

NINE

Iron Eyes felt the cool forest soothing his skin as he guided the lathered-up horse between the tall, straight pine trees. It had taken him a long time to reach this forest and he still had no idea why he was in this place.

But wherever this pine-scented haven was, it was better than anywhere else Iron Eyes had been in a long while. The air tasted good here. Sweeter than the air out in the blinding sun-scorched prairie. Iron Eyes touched his scalp and tried to force his fingernails into the stitches. He could still not feel anything along the top of his head, yet the drumming inside his skull persisted.

Would the pain ever stop? The throbbing noise inside his head was like a hundred war drums continually pounding. He inhaled the cool, fragrant air into his narrow nostrils and felt better than he had since the deadly encounter

67

with Dan Creedy. Iron Eyes had been like a wounded animal seeking a place to heal itself since the fight back in the saloon at Bonny. As he inhaled the cool air into his lungs, he knew this forest held the answers he sought.

As the snorting mount stepped into an ice-cold stream, Iron Eyes allowed the exhausted animal to stop, lower its head and drink. The bounty hunter stared around the gloomy forest interior, trying to decide on a route which would allow him to relax in his saddle. There were many choices, but one caught his keen eyes. The shafts of sunlight seemed to point at a trail which gradually rose through the countless straight trees to a higher place. Iron Eyes knew that was where he would head.

It had been so many years since he had entered such a place as this cool, fresh forest. The last time was so far back in his grim past that he could not recall it in any detail. All he knew for sure was when he had last lived in such a place, there had been no human blood on his hands.

Back then Iron Eyes had hunted creatures. Only creatures. Long before he had changed into the ruthless manhunter who was feared throughout the west.

His keen ears heard the rustling of animals as they moved unseen through the tall vegetation. Birds sang out cheerfully from almost every tree branch around him, as if greeting the ominous visitor to their home. There was plenty of game in this forest, he thought, as he spied a deer running through a clearing not more than twenty feet from his horse.

Iron Eyes ran his long, thin fingers across his brow as if trying to purge his head of the pain that continually reminded him of his wound. The war drums started again as the veins on his temple began throbbing.

For a moment he had thought the sounds were coming from some unseen Indians readying themselves for war, but then realized it was all in his head. Iron Eyes rose in his saddle and slowly dismounted. His mule-ear boots became cool as the icy water passed continuously over them on its way to another place. Holding on to his saddle fender as if unsure of his ability to balance, Iron Eyes leaned over and scooped some of the clear liquid up in the palm of his hand and tasted it.

It was good. It tasted the way water was meant to taste. Pure. This was not the muddy well-water served up in the towns he had ridden through for half his life, but was cold and refreshing.

Removing his canteen from the saddle horn, Iron Eyes unscrewed its stopper and poured out the contents before lowering it into the water and allowing the flowing water to fill it. When it was filled, he raised it to his lips and began drinking.

He did not stop until he had consumed the entire contents. He was still giddy, but now felt the pain inside his skull easing as if cleansed by a magical potion.

Iron Eyes lowered the canteen into the stream again and refilled it. Then he firmly secured its stopper. He felt the cold liquid moving down through his body. It felt good. For the first time since the elderly doctor had sewn his head back together the pain was noticeably easing.

Iron Eyes hung the canteen back on the saddle horn and stepped into his stirrup before hauling his long, lean frame back into the saddle. He allowed the horse to continue drinking its fill until it raised its head. Then he tapped his spurs into the flesh of the animal once again. The mount began to walk.

Aiming at the long shafts of sun, Iron Eyes rode on up the trail. This time he would allow the tired horse to find its own pace. He was no longer in a hurry.

For the first time since he had started hunting men instead of animals, Iron Eyes actually felt at peace. There was no longer any reason to rush. This was a place where reward money was of no value and a man lived or died by his skill at hunting. Once he had regained all his senses, Iron Eyes told himself that he would rekindle all his old skills.

The Fury of Iron Eyes

He could taste the succulent flavours of fresh game as his memory reminded him of the last time he had eaten something he had caught.

As the long legs of his mount slowly navigated along the cool mountain trail, the bounty hunter wrapped his leather reins around his wrists and closed his eyes. The horse continued walking on up the trail with its master slumped in his saddle.

For the first time in countless days, Iron Eyes allowed himself to sleep.

TEN

The sun was low in the sky when the three Creedy brothers thundered into the small town of Bonny. They had purchased fresh mounts before leaving Tequila Flats, and ridden them into the ground to reach Bonny as quickly as possible. The dust seemed to linger in the air long after the three riders had dragged their reins up to their chests and stopped their exhausted mounts outside the solitary saloon.

The elderly sheriff had watched the three horsemen dismounting outside the saloon and knew this might be the day he had dreaded since first taking office. This might be the day when he had to earn his meagre pay cheque.

The three remaining Creedy brothers did not stay in the saloon very long, and were soon out on the street again glancing around at the weathered structures, searching for something or some-

72

one to confront. It did not take long for them to notice the feeble law officer standing outside his office.

The sheriff felt his heart beginning to pound beneath his undershirt as the men started walking directly at him. He knew these faces. They had been here many times before with their brother Dan Creedy. He had always known who they were and had never done anything to force their hand.

Unlike the sheriff, these men were neither old nor afraid. They were deadly killers like their dead brother and the shaking lawman wanted no part of them. They reached the porch of his office and stopped in a line before him. Even saddle-weary, they were a formidable sight.

'Sheriff,' Bob Creedy said touching the wide brim of Stetson in greeting.

'I wondered when you boys would get here,' the sheriff said in a feeble voice that told the trio he would do nothing to prevent them going about their business – whatever it was.

'They ain't had time to wash Dan's blood off the floor in the saloon, Sheriff,' Bob Creedy said in a tone that hovered on the very edge of fury.

'Most of that blood belongs to Iron Eyes, boys,' the sheriff informed the men.

Treat Creedy stepped forward and stared hard into the face of the frightened man.

'Iron Eyes was wounded?'

'Dan almost took the varmint's head off his shoulders,' the lawman nodded as he noticed the men's mood altering.

The three faces suddenly began to smile.

'I told you that Dan wouldn't go down without shooting back,' Bob Creedy told his brothers.

'Where's Iron Eyes now?' Frankie Creedy asked.

'He high-tailed it out of here a few days back,' the sheriff replied. 'As soon as he got his reward money.'

'Blood money!' Frankie spat.

'I thought you said this Iron Eyes critter was wounded, Sheriff?' Treat queried. 'How could he leave Bonny with his head half shot off?'

'He was wounded, son. Never seen a man so close to death and still able to ride.' The lawman felt sweat rolling down his spine as he leaned on a wooden upright in a vain attempt to stop his entire body from shaking.

'Which way did he head, Sheriff?' Bob asked.

'Towards the pine forests.' The sheriff pointed a trembling finger. 'I figure his trail should be easy to follow considering he's the only rider to head out that way in over a month of Sundays.'

'We'll catch the murderer,' Treat vowed quietly as he stared in the direction that the lawman had gestured.

'How come he went that way? What's over there?' Frankie was curious. He had roamed this range for several years and knew there were no towns anywhere close to the forested hills. There was nothing out there to lure a bounty hunter or anyone else for that matter.

The sheriff looked at the ground. 'Ain't nothing in them forests except a whole bunch of Indians.'

The three brothers looked at one another for a few seconds, as if trying to work out the motives of a man they had only just become aware of as being more than just a legend.

'Indians? What sort of Indians, Sheriff?' Bob questioned.

The sheriff swallowed hard. 'Cheyenne. They got themselves a reservation in the mountains someplace beyond the forest. I ain't too sure 'cos I ain't never been there. No sane man has.'

There was a silence as the dust-caked men tried to work out why Iron Eyes had headed towards a place which offered no profit to him.

'Maybe he's trying to throw us off his trail,' Frankie suggested to his brothers. 'Maybe he figures we'll be following him and get scared at going into Cheyenne territory.'

'That could be it,' Treat nodded.

'I ain't scared of no redskins,' Frankie snorted. 'I want to get my hands on this bastard they call Iron Eyes.'

Suddenly Treat Creedy noticed the face of their older brother as he stood rubbing his whiskers thoughtfully. He moved to the pale-skinned Bob's side and just looked at him.

'Where's Dan's body, Sheriff?' Bob mumbled solemnly up at the old man.

'Up in the undertakers, boy.' The sheriff pointed his finger at the wooden structure a hundred yards away. 'I made sure he was laid out right.'

'Thanks, Sheriff,' Bob swallowed. 'Much obliged for your kindness.'

The three men turned and began walking down the street towards the small building. Their pace was slower now as they closed down the distance between themselves and the undertakers. None of the brothers wanted to see Dan lying lifelessly in a wooden box, but knew they had to do so.

Until they set eyes upon the corpse, there was still hope that it might not be Dan who had been gunned down by the mysterious Iron Eyes. A few seconds after entering the building, they knew there had been no mistake. Dan was dead. Less than a minute after walking back into the street again, they had mounted their horses and headed out of Bonny.

The sheriff had been correct. The trail left by Iron Eyes's horse was easy to follow. The three riders spurred their mounts on.

ELEVEN

Sergeant John Walker held on tightly to his Springfield rifle and studied the tree-covered hills which loomed over the small encampment. He had been in many such situations during his twenty or so years in the service of Old Glory, but had never quite felt as helpless as he did at this very moment.

The troopers who had been told to dig in knew nothing of what lay out there beyond the shimmering grass. They had no notion of the fact that they were at least five miles within the boundaries of the Cheyenne reservation. They sat in the holes they had been ordered to dig, clutching their single shot rifles, trying to work out why.

The burly sergeant bit off another mouthful of chewing tobacco and slowly began to grind it down into a pulp with what was left of his teeth.

Every few minutes he would spit out a lump of black saliva and then continue.

He alone among the enlisted men knew what was out there. He alone was privileged to the thoughts of his troubled superior, and yet he wished his mind was as innocent as the young troopers. They did not know what horrors might be waiting to befall them. As Walker spat again, he glanced at the major before returning his attention to the trees.

Major Thomas Roberts sat beneath a proud oak and waited for inspiration; it seemed unwilling to visit him. He knew he had drawn the short straw when sent on this suicidal mission, yet could not think of a way out of it.

Bull Fergis was not a happy man as he strode through the tall grass towards the brooding officer. There seemed no words which could be spoken that would calm down the irate gold miner. Roberts did not attempt any as the well-built man stopped above him.

'Well?' Fergis growled with his clenched fists resting on his hips.

'The daylight is almost gone, Mr Fergis. So far it seems that we have not been spotted,' Roberts sighed.

'We ought to cut out of here by now,' Bull Fergis said as he leaned down until their noses were almost touching. 'I've spoken to all my men and they want to get out of here. To hell with the gold.'

Major Roberts nodded. 'I agree, but there is something you forget.'

Fergis's face went blank as he straightened up trying to think of what the army officer meant.

Thomas Roberts rose to his feet and looked across at his men waiting in their shallow ditches. Slowly he turned and stared down into the harsh features of the gold miner.

'You boys have your orders and I've got mine. If I disobey mine I'll be kicked out of the army, and if you break your contract with the mining company, you and your men will probably be sued.'

Bull Fergis scratched at his long beard. 'But we was lied to by the agent, Major.'

'I was told the truth,' Roberts said. 'The trouble is, I was given no alternative than to lead this insane mission. If I take you boys back to Fort Bruce, they'll nail my hide to the wall.'

'So you'll risk keeping us all here just to save your damn career?' Fergis snarled loudly.

Major Roberts noticed the faces of his young troopers looking in his direction. Their trust was being betrayed by his own selfishness. They deserved better than to be waiting for certain death, he thought. Yet this was the fate he was preparing them for.

'You're absolutely right, Mr Fergis. Let us try and get out of here before sunset.'

Fergis snorted and nodded violently. 'You figure we've got time?'

'If you get your oxen hitched up to your wagons as fast as possible, there is a chance we can slip back out of here before the Cheyenne spot us,' Major Roberts said as he tried to remain calm.

The large shadow of Sergeant Walker covered both men as he walked up to them. As their faces looked up into his, they both noticed the pained expression carved in his features.

'What is it, John?' Roberts asked fearfully.

The big sergeant aimed the barrel of his Springfield rifle up at the hills to their right and then waved it like a fan. Both the gold miner and the officer went silent as they saw the plumes of smoke rising from at least five points along the forested hills.

'Reckon they've spotted us, sir.'

'What are we gonna do, Major?' Fergis raged.

Roberts kicked at the ground and then turned away. He had no answers to give either man.

TWELVE

He could have been no more than sixteen summers old, yet had a nobility far beyond his years. There was a beauty in the clean features of the youthful rider that transcended race. His skin was no darker than the average tanned cowboy out on the Texas range, yet his braided hair laced with two eagle feathers and immaculate beaded-buckskin clothing made it obvious, even from a distance, that this was a Cheyenne brave.

Astride a highly-decorated gelded grey pony, the youthful rider had silently been moving up through the mountainous forest trails for several days. The peaceful reservation of the Southern Cheyenne held no challenges for his kind to prove themselves as in earlier times.

The rituals of days gone by had died with the last of the Indian wars, and were no longer demanded by the tribal elders. Now, young bucks did not have to have the talons of an eagle skewered through their chest and be hung by rawhide ropes until the Great Spirit pronounced them warriors. They no longer had to seek out and take the heart of their enemies to prove their manhood.

For braves such as the one who rose up through the tall straight trees in search of game, the old days were but a memory he had heard others talk about around the camp fires.

They had called him Silent Wolf. As he had grown into his early manhood, the name seemed more and more accurate. The Cheyenne brave had few equals when it came to hunting, and the elders wondered whether he was capable of changing into a real wolf when he was out in the hills and mountains searching for fresh game.

Surely, they mused, only a real 'silent wolf' could have managed to hunt so successfully. Many other braves wanted to ride with the young Cheyenne when he went hunting, but Silent Wolf always rode alone.

Even at his tender age, Silent Wolf had become almost legendary amongst his own people. For in the folklore of the Cheyenne, as well as other tribes of the plains, it was said that certain Indians possessed the ability to change into animals whenever they wished. It was a gift, bestowed by the Great Spirit.

Whatever the truth of it, Silent Wolf was differ-

ent to the majority of his people. He kept himself
to himself and preferred to ride alone through the
majestic forests whenever possible.

As the grey pony reached the summit of the tall
trail, the Indian dragged at the animal's mane.
The mount stopped and its master stared wide-
eyed at the sight before him. Silent Wolf had
ridden this route countless times before seeking
deer and other game, but his keen eyes had never
witnessed anything like the horrific vision before
him in the dying rays of the sun.

For a brief moment, the young Cheyenne had
thought he was looking at one of his own people
lying on the ground, at the feet of the tall, nervous
horse. Silent Wolf squinted in the half-light down
at the wrists of the fallen rider. They were still
wrapped in the reins, keeping the animal from
fleeing. The warrior knew that must have been
why the mount had not deserted its master.

Perhaps it was the long, black hair which
cascaded over the collar of his stained coat which
had made Silent Wolf think he was looking at the
body of one of his fellow Cheyenne. It had only
taken a few moments for the young rider to realize that whoever this was lying on the ground, he
was not an Indian.

Throwing a leg over the neck of his grey pony,
Silent Wolf slid to the ground and began advancing towards the motionless figure.

With each step he took, Silent Wolf felt his heart beating faster. As he stood a few feet from the stretched-out figure, he noticed the terrible wound which appeared to go from the front of the man's skull to the crown. Silent Wolf had never seen such a wound, not such an example of the white man's medicine. The stitches still held Iron Eyes's scalp together, but were seeping blood.

The Indian drew his long knife from his belt and held it tightly as he knelt down beside the crumpled body. With his free hand he touched Iron Eyes. There was no reaction.

Silent Wolf had met few white men during his life, but none of them had looked anything like Iron Eyes. The mane of black hair confused the Cheyenne as he moved around the figure trying to work out whether he was still alive.

He had no knowledge of white men having hair as long as his own. As he turned the face away from the ground, Silent Wolf studied the scarred features. The face looked like none he had ever seen before. It did not look like that of any Indian he had heard of, and yet it did not look like a white man's either. Neither did it look like the face of someone of mixed race.

What had he discovered? What breed of man was this lying on the ground beside him?

Silent Wolf was curious yet nervous. He, like the rest of his people, had a thousand legends, and the warrior's brain raced as he wondered if this strange manifestation fitted any of the tales he had been told.

Then Iron Eyes grunted. The young Cheyenne recoiled backwards in shock as he realized who or whatever this man was, he was still alive. It seemed impossible to the skilled Indian hunter that anyone in such condition could be anything but dead, yet the man was now groaning.

Silent Wolf jumped to his feet and stared hard at Iron Eyes, as the bounty hunter rolled over on to his side and finally opened his eyes.

The two men looked fixedly at one another. The sky had gone red above them as the sun set, and filled the small clearing in a haunting crimson light.

Neither seemed very sure of what they were looking at.

THIRTEEN

Darkness had come only a few minutes after the three riders had reached the forest and entered following the trail left by Iron Eyes's horse. There was a chilling terror in this place which overwhelmed the three Creedys.

They halted their mounts and waited for a sign. There was none. Bob Creedy seemed first to be able to see what surrounded them and dismounted. Faint echoes of a large moon somehow managed to penetrate the canopy of branches above them and filtered into the forest interior. Its eerie light chilled their bones.

'What you doing, Bob?' Treat Creedy asked his brother as the older man walked slowly around their horses, studying the ground.

'Looking for tracks,' Bob replied.

'It's kinda dark to see any tracks, Bob,' Frankie snapped angrily as he watched the shimmering moonlight creating horrific images all around them – images he knew were simply tricks of the poor light, yet made the hair on the nape of his neck stand on end.

'I can see good enough,' Bob replied as he knelt down on the moist ground. 'Iron Eyes headed up that way.'

Treat and Frankie stared in the direction their older brother was pointing, at the trail which rose up through the tall, black tree trunks.

'Are you sure?' Treat asked as he watched Bob stepping into his stirrup and mounting his horse.

Gathering his reins in his hands, Bob nodded and gently spurred his horse. As he slowly allowed the creature to walk up the narrow trail he called back, 'You coming?'

The two riders spurred their own horses and followed.

Iron Eyes sat curiously in the dirt watching the young Cheyenne brave. Silent Wolf watched him with equal intensity. Even after the sunlight had made way for the bright moon, the two hunters just watched one another from a safe distance in the mountain-top clearing.

They seemed in awe of each other. The young warrior had never seen anyone so badly injured before. Someone obviously at his lowest ebb, yet defiantly clinging to life. For his part, Iron Eyes had never been so close to an Indian who looked so positively regal before.

Both could not believe what they were looking at. Silent Wolf wondered if this strange creature was perhaps a demon who had taken human form, for Iron Eyes appeared unlike any man the young Indian had ever seen before.

Iron Eyes was still unsure whether or not his pounding brain was simply playing tricks on him. He had heard tell of men who had suffered head injuries and spent the rest of their days seeing things which were not really there. The bounty hunter wondered if he, too, had succumbed to insanity, or perhaps was merely dreaming.

The bright moon bathed the seated warrior in a glowing light that certainly did not seem real, Iron Eyes thought. For more than ten minutes Silent Wolf had not moved a muscle as he sat cross-legged beside his pony looking at him.

Finally, Iron Eyes cleared his throat and spoke. 'Are you really there?'

Silent Wolf said nothing for a few seconds, then nodded.

'You understand my lingo,' Silent Wolf muttered in a low voice which testified to the fact that although still young, he had left his boyhood behind him.

'What happened?'

'Me find you.'

'I figured that much.' Iron Eyes touched his scalp and for the first time since being shot by Dan Creedy, felt agonizing pain racing over his stitched wound. Wincing, the bounty hunter suddenly realized that this was not a dream, but real. The small spots of blood on his fingertips bore testament to that.

'You hurt bad,' Silent Wolf said pointing his knife at his own head. 'Man should die with such wound. Why you not die?'

Iron Eyes began to clamber to his feet. 'Maybe I'm just stubborn.'

'Me no understand,' Silent Wolf said as he watched the tall, thin figure of the strange man before him.

Iron Eyes steadied himself as he looked at the handsome Cheyenne.

'I'm too bad to die. When you're dead you either have to go to heaven or hell. I reckon neither place wants me.'

Silent Wolf nodded as if agreeing with the statement.

'What tribe you belong?'

Iron Eyes removed the canteen from his saddle and unscrewed the stopper as he pondered the question. It was one he had asked himself many times during his life. Raising the canteen to his dry lips and drinking the cold water, he wondered what the answer was. For all his days, he had never seemed to fit in with any of the numerous people that filled the west. If he had ever had parents, he could not recall them. His first memories were of his hunting in a forest. He had always been alone. He had always killed one creature or another.

'You have tribe?' Silent Wolf asked again.

'I ain't too sure, friend,' Iron Eyes replied as he raised the canteen and felt the cooling water filtering down inside his body. 'I've always been alone. Guess no tribe would have me for one of their own.'

The Cheyenne seemed interested and stood up. 'You like being on own?'

'Never had much choice.' Iron Eyes offered the canteen to the wary youth and nodded when it was accepted. He watched as the Cheyenne drank and then returned the canteen.

'You white man?'

Iron Eyes shrugged. 'I ain't too sure.'

There seemed to be no fear in the young Cheyenne as he began to edge around the curiosity he had discovered. Above all things, Silent Wolf could not help but be amazed at the height of Iron Eyes. It was like being in the presence of a giant.

'You must be Indian,' Silent Wolf said before reconsidering his words. 'But no Indian tall like trees. What your name?'

'They call me Iron Eyes,' the bounty hunter answered.

'I am called Silent Wolf. I great hunter.'

'I'm a hunter too, Silent Wolf,' Iron Eyes smiled.

'The Great Spirit has brought two hunters together,' Silent Wolf said as he pointed his gleaming knife at the moon.

'Where are we, little hunter?' Iron Eyes asked as he hung the canteen back on his saddlehorn and stared out at the moonlit scenery.

'This Cheyenne land,' Silent Wolf replied.

Iron Eyes's head turned and looked down at the handsome face.

'The whole damn thing belongs to the Cheyenne?'

The brave nodded. 'We have treaty.'

'If they're all as hospitable as you, I'll be OK.' Iron Eyes rubbed his aching head as he leaned on the saddle. 'If not, I'm in a mighty bad pickle.'

'Me no understand.'

'It don't matter none,' Iron Eyes sighed.

FOURTEEN

Night had quickly found the valley where Major Thomas Roberts was encamped with his hundred troopers and the gold miners. Yet the hours of night were not to bring them any security due to the brilliant moon which had replaced the blazing sun. Roberts knew they required a black sky if they were to make a successful retreat from this dangerous place. The officer could still see the smoke rising from the forested hills against the hazy night sky, but now he could also make out the flames which were being fanned.

They were being warned to get off the reservation of the Southern Cheyenne and Major Roberts intended to heed that warning. There was no glory in fighting a foe when you knew, with every sinew of your being, that it was you who were in the wrong.

Roberts prayed that he still had time to get his

caravan of miners, wagons and troopers out of the valley before sun-up. He also prayed that he had not left it too late.

A sound began to chill his entire company as they remained in their shallow ditches. It was a sound that had not filled the officer's ears for many years, but it haunted his memory. It was the sound of distant drumming echoing around the dark hills of trees. It was impossible to tell where the drumming was coming from, but wherever it was originating, it seemed to be getting louder with every passing second.

'Are we gonna be attacked by Indians, Major?' one of the troopers asked Roberts as he walked slowly along the line of men in their foxholes.

'Easy, son,' Roberts's calm voice soothed.

Bull Fergis rushed from his wagons up to the major and gasped as he spoke.

'My boys have hitched up all the oxen to the wagons. We're ready and able to skedaddle out of here when you've a mind to give the order.'

'Good.' Roberts patted the man on his solid shoulder as he walked through the long, moist grass to where Sergeant Walker was waiting. 'Are the horses saddled and readied, John?'

'Like you ordered, sir,' Walker nodded.

Thomas Roberts removed his white gauntlets from his black belt and pulled them on to his hands.

'Gentlemen, we have to do this properly if we are to escape with our hair. We must make a quiet evacuation of this place. It is obvious that we are being watched and the Cheyenne could strike at any time, but I think they will allow us to leave their land peacefully.'

'I heard tell that Injuns don't attack at night, Major,' Bull Fergis said.

'I'm afraid that is not exactly accurate, Mr Fergis,' Roberts informed the miner.

'It ain't?'

'It ain't!' Walker grunted.

'I suggest you offload as much heavy tools and machinery as possible from your wagons,' Roberts instructed Fergis.

'But all our money is tied up in our equipment,' Bull Fergis protested. 'We can't just dump it.'

'It will slow you and us up, Mr Fergis,' Roberts said in a stern voice.

'But it's valuable,' Fergis protested.

'More valuable than your hair?'

'My hair?' Bull Fergis's eyes widened as he looked into the face of the officer. It was a face with very last bit of humour drained from it. 'What ya mean?'

'I could be wrong about the mood of the Cheyenne. They might be just boiling over to have a fight with us, Mr Fergis,' Major Roberts sighed. 'Oxen don't run very fast at the best of times, let alone when they are pulling heavy wagons.'

'What about the explosives?' Bull Fergis swallowed hard as he suddenly began to realize that
their escape from this lush valley was by no
means a certainty.

'Keep all your weaponry, liquor and explosives
on your wagons, Mr Fergis,' Roberts advised. 'We
do not want them falling into the wrong hands, do
we?'

It was a pale-faced Fergis who turned around
towards his fellow miners.

'We'd better strip some of the heavy equipment
off the wagons, boys. We might have to make a run
for it.'

Roberts leaned closer to his burly sergeant.

'Get a dozen troopers and bring all our horses
here. I do not wish to waste a single second when
the miners have stripped some weight off their
wagons.'

'Right away, Major.' Walker touched the brim of
his hat. Then he ran along the line of troopers
lying on their bellies and gathered enough men
together to accomplish his orders.

Thomas Roberts knew that if the Cheyenne
were to attack, they would not ride at his men
offering themselves as target, but crawl through
the long grass unseen and then strike.

For all Roberts knew, they were already doing
just that.

FIFTEEN

The tall, ghost-like figure of Iron Eyes stepped to the very edge of the clearing and stared down at the vast, tree-covered scenery below him. He was suddenly nervous.

'What wrong, Iron Eyes?' Silent Wolf asked.

'You smell smoke?'

'Yes,' Silent Wolf nodded as he sniffed the air. 'Fire!'

Both men tried to work out where the burning scent was coming from as they moved around the lip of a sheer drop. Then the young Cheyenne pointed to their right. Even though it was still night, the moonlight showed the dark swirling clouds drifting on the still air.

'There. See?'

'Yep. I see it OK. Is it a forest fire, Silent Wolf?' Iron Eyes asked his companion.

'No. Smoke come from many signal fires.'

Iron Eyes looked perplexed. 'I don't get it.'

'Smoke signals. Warning of intruders,' the young Cheyenne added as he gestured with his hands, the way many plains tribes communicated to one another when unsure of the other's dialect.

'Maybe your people noticed me.' The bounty hunter moved away from the sheer drop and studied his newly-found friend. It was something he found awkward as he had never felt the emotion of friendship before. 'Maybe I got them all riled up.'

'Not you. Must be others. Many others.' Silent Wolf moved back to his pony. 'Smoke only used when our land is violated by outsiders.'

'What do you mean by outsiders, little hunter?' Iron Eyes gazed at the handsome Indian curiously.

'My people only make smoke signals when army or other big enemy enters reservation, Iron Eyes,' the youth explained.

'What would soldiers want to enter your reservation for?'

'This land has the yellow stones white men like.'

'You mean gold?' Iron Eyes had never understood why so many men seemed to lose their sanity when it came to gold. To him it was worthless unless made into a golden eagle coin.

'Yes. Gold.' The Cheyenne threw himself on to the back of his mount and gathered up the crude, rawhide-rope rein with one hand as his other held the animal's mane.

'Maybe we ought to go take a look at what's gotten your people so worked up, Silent Wolf,' Iron Eyes said through gritted teeth as he moved towards his horse.

'We go and see,' the Cheyenne hunter nodded as he expertly controlled his pony.

Iron Eyes raised an eyebrow. 'Is it healthy for me to be seen by your tribe?'

'You safe with me. They not harm friend of Silent Wolf.'

Reluctantly, Iron Eyes stepped into his stirrup and hauled himself atop his horse.

'OK. But if they start shooting at me, I'll shoot back.'

'They say man never see or hear bullet or arrow that kill him, Iron Eyes,' Silent Wolf said as he turned his pony around.

'Maybe so, but I'll kill the varmint who kills me.' Iron Eyes stared at the brave Cheyenne and nudged his mount closer. There was something about the Indian which intrigued the battle-scarred bounty hunter. Perhaps he reminded him of himself at that age. 'Are you as good a hunter as you look, Silent Wolf?'

'There are those who say I am blessed by the Great Spirit and able to turn into a real wolf whenever I wish,' Silent Wolf said calmly.

'Is it true?'

'Maybe true. Maybe not true.'

'You teasing a fellow hunter, Silent Wolf?' Iron Eyes gave the young brave a long, knowing look.

'Me no understand, Iron Eyes.' The Cheyenne almost smiled as he kicked his heels into the sides of his pony and started down the overgrown trail.

'The hell you don't.'

The smell of smoke filled the bounty hunter's nostrils as he gathered up his loose reins. Suddenly Iron Eyes was reminded that he and Silent Wolf were not alone in this vast forest.

Iron Eyes tapped his spurs into the flesh of his horse and began to follow the young brave into the black shadows. He had heard of the legends which told of certain Indians being able to turn into animals and birds at will. Until now, he had thought they were just tall tales, yet Iron Eyes knew there was something different about the elegant Cheyenne he was following. If there was an Indian capable of transforming into another creature, it was Silent Wolf, Iron Eyes thought.

As the bounty hunter's tall horse followed the grey pony deeper and deeper along the dark, narrow trail which wound its way between the straight pine trees, Iron Eyes knew in his guts that they were heading into a place he had been to many times. A place called trouble.

SIXTEEN

'There!' Silent Wolf pointed as the two riders reached another clearing halfway down the steep mountain trail. 'See them, Iron Eyes? Soldiers!'

'I see them, Silent Wolf,' Iron Eyes growled as he focused on the valley below their high vantage point. Even the moonlight could not disguise the white-canvas-topped wagons and scores of mounted cavalry milling around in the valley of swaying grass. 'What the hell are them soldier boys doing there? If this is an Indian reservation, they got no right to even enter.'

'They on Cheyenne land. Why?' Silent Wolf asked angrily as he pulled his ancient rifle from its hiding place inside a large hide bag, hanging across the shoulders of his pony.

'Reckon it must be something to do with the gold you told me about, little hunter.' Iron Eyes held his reins high to his chest as he balanced in his stirrups watching the activity below. 'A lot of white folks would skin their mothers to get hold of a few ounces of gold.'

Silent Wolf raised his rifle and nestled its wooden stock against his shoulder, whilst looking down its length trying to line up its rusty sights.

'I kill white men.'

'No! You can't just start killing troopers.' Iron Eyes reached across and pushed the barrel down.

'Why, Iron Eyes?'

'Cos it would give them critters an excuse to attack your people, Silent Wolf,' Iron Eyes reasoned. He had seen it happen many times. 'That sort don't need any excuse to kill more Indians.'

Suddenly Silent Wolf aimed his index finger at the densely-wooded hill opposite the one they were on.

'Big trouble coming.'

Iron Eyes could see what the young brave was talking about as he stared in the direction his companion was indicating. At first it just looked like spots of light moving in a long line through a forest trail. Then, Iron Eyes realized it was the light of the large moon catching the raised war-lances and rifles of hundreds of Cheyenne riders as they made their way to a point above the encamped soldiers.

'Looks like them soldiers are in for a fight.' Iron

Eyes ran his fingers through his mane of black hair and felt the pain of his stitched-up scalp. His head still ached but he no longer heard the throbbing drumming inside his skull. The only drumming he heard now was coming from somewhere below in the heartland of the Cheyenne as their warriors advanced on the cavalry.

'Why soldiers want gold?' the young brave asked his grim-faced companion.

'Greed,' Iron Eyes muttered under his breath.

'No understand,' Silent Wolf said as he looked back into the stony features of the bounty hunter. 'What is greed?'

'It's when one man wants what another man has,' Iron Eyes informed.

'You mean they want Cheyenne gold?'

Iron Eyes nudged his horse closer to the younger man's pony. 'They probably want your entire reservation as well.'

'That is wrong,' Silent Wolf breathed heavily as his chest heaved. 'My people would give them the yellow rocks if they asked, for it is of no use. Gold is not strong enough make knife. It is heavy. It useless.'

'But it shines,' Iron Eyes shrugged. 'Folks back east like it 'cos it shines.'

'They stupid.' The young Cheyenne spat at the ground.

'They sure ain't got the same values as us

103

hunters and that's for sure, Silent Wolf.' Iron Eyes watched as the distant warriors continued past the soldiers and headed towards the mouth of the valley. He was curious. 'Where are your people headed?'

'I do not know,' Silent Wolf replied as he, too, wondered where his fellow Cheyenne were going. As a hunter, he would have stopped when he was above his prey and then struck. Seeing the long line of Indian riders continuing through the trees made no sense to his own honed instincts.

Before either man could speak again, a noise like thunderous lightning bolts filled both their ears. The red-hot tapers of bullets seemed to flash all around them from behind their mounts.

They were being shot at.

Without knowing what or who could be using them for target practice, Iron Eyes slapped his long reins across the tail of Silent Wolf's grey pony. The animal leapt forward and raced through a gap between the trees with its young master hanging on to its mane. Iron Eyes swung his horse full-circle as the shots tore up the air around him, and drew one of his Navy Colts. He fired blindly back at the place where the bullets were originating.

As Iron Eyes's sixth bullet blasted from the long blue barrel of his pistol, he turned the horse and dug his spurs into its flesh. The animal jumped down on to the lower ground where the grey pony had just fled, and then began to follow.

Pushing his empty gun into one of his roomy coat pockets, Iron Eyes grabbed his reins in both hands, pulled his mount's head up and rode into the darkness.

Bullets continued to follow the bounty hunter until he managed to steer his petrified horse into the dense trees. He continued riding hard until he saw the waiting Cheyenne rider before him. Only then did he drag his mount to a stop.

'Who shoot at us, Iron Eyes?'

Iron Eyes dismounted and checked his horse before replying. 'Whoever it was, they were using handguns.'

'How you know this?'

'I've heard most guns in my time, little hunter. That was two Remingtons and a Colt.' Iron Eyes ran his hand over his tired horse and bit his lip.

'Must be white men,' Silent Wolf said thoughtfully. 'But why white men up here and why they shoot at us?'

'I figure they was shooting at me.' Iron Eyes shook his head as he felt the pain starting once again inside his skull. The violent riding had also started his head wound bleeding again and a thin line of blood trickled down his face. The bounty hunter ran a finger across his temple and stared at the blood on it.

'You bleeding.'

'Yeah,' Iron Eyes said whilst loading his empty gun before ramming it into his belt next to its lethal twin. 'I keep bleeding like this and there ain't gonna be none left.'

'Who shoot at Iron Eyes and Silent Wolf?' the brave asked out loud.

Iron Eyes tied his reins to a tree branch. 'Reckon I ought to take a look.'

Silent Wolf leapt from his pony and ran to the side of the gaunt figure. 'We both take look.'

Iron Eyes was in no mood to argue. 'Let's do us some tracking, little hunter.'

SEVENTEEN

The sound of distant gunfire was still echoing all around the moonlit valley, and in the hearts of the cavalry who waited anxiously for the gold miners to ready their ten wagons. There was a chilling warning to the troopers in the sounds of the bullets that came from the mountainous forests.

It was clear that something had or was still occurring in the black trees above his men, and Major Roberts decided he could wait no longer to make his retreat from this handsome valley. Bullets were being fired and the officer had no idea who their intended targets were. He stepped into his stirrup, hauled himself on to his fresh, eager mount and rode around his men trying to impart his own stalwart courage into his meagre force.

Major Thomas Roberts grabbed hold of his reins and eased his horse towards the large figure of Sergeant Walker.

'Let's get out of this place, John.'

'Reckon it must be about time, sir,' Walker
nodded in obedience.

'Hopefully we have not left it too late,' Roberts
whispered to his favourite soldier.

The burly sergeant screamed at the troopers to
mount whilst Roberts rode along the line of
wagons until he found the one with Bull Fergis
sitting on its driving board. Reining in, the officer
leaned close to the wheel brake and spoke to the
bearded man.

'I hope you're ready, Mr Fergis, because I'm
heading out right now. Those shots might not
have been aimed directly at us, but I for one am
not going to wait for the second volley.'

Fergis wrestled with the heavy reins attached
to his team of oxen and nodded. 'We're ready,
Major. You lead and we'll follow.'

'I pray we shall live to share a bottle of whiskey
together, Mr Fergis.' Roberts waved his white
gauntlet in the air and then rode ahead of the
caravan entrusted to his care. One by one the
wagons began to move slowly through the tall,
damp grass after the straight-backed officer,
whilst the troopers flanked them on both sides.

It was a slow-moving company of vehicles and
riders at first, which gradually increased its pace
as the heavy oxen managed to find their footing in
the fertile soil.

Sergeant Walker drove his mount through the long grass until he was next to the horse of Major Roberts. It was the place that he always chose to be.

'What do you reckon those shots were all about, sir?' Walker asked his leader.

'I'm not sure, but I'm in no hurry to find out either. All I want to do is get out of this valley and back on the prairie before there's trouble,' the officer announced, as he allowed his horse to canter at a pace designed to allow the wagons to catch up with him.

'Sounded like a gunfight to me,' Walker said as he kept his horse level with Roberts's.

'You might be correct, but we have other things to do tonight rather than theorize about that.' Roberts looked back at the wagons as their drivers were managing to get their huge teams of oxen to gain speed. The sound of bullwhips cracking above the horns of the teams of massive oxen echoed around the valley. It was a sound which chilled the riding troopers as their tired eyes scanned the forested hills for signs of trouble.

'Guess you're right, sir. We gotta try and get this band of misfits to safety,' Walker shouted as he held on to his reins and rode alongside the troubled commander of their aborted mission.

The grim-faced officer knew the words of his faithful sergeant were harsh but true. These men, who rode on horses and wagons, knew nothing of Indian fighting. They had not fought for their very lives as he and Walker had done so long ago. They were placing their lives in his hands. They could do nothing but have faith that he would make the correct decisions and not lead them to their deaths.

As Thomas Roberts guided his trotting horse ever onward, he hoped that he still had all the skills this duty warranted for success. He prayed with every stride of his mount, that he still remembered enough of the ways of the Cheyenne to return these terrified followers to the safety of Fort Bruce.

They continued along the valley, bathed in the haunting blue light of the large, taunting moon above them until they had covered nearly three miles. It had been an uneventful retreat, which every soul under the command of Major Roberts was grateful for, but it was not to remain that way.

Suddenly, ahead of the hundred riders and the ten wagons, Major Roberts caught sight of something which at first he imagined was merely an apparition.

As he led them closer to what he had thought to be a trick of the light, Roberts realized it was real.

EIGHTEEN

Never in all his days had Major Thomas Roberts ever witnessed a sight more terrifying than the one which confronted him as he rode along the valley ahead of the goldminers' wagons and his troopers. This was something he had not expected in his wildest nightmares.

Visible in the haunting light of the large moon Roberts could clearly see a barricade directly ahead of them. It was a wall of tinder-dry brush that had been dragged from the forest and spread across the narrow mouth of the lush valley.

Aiming his spirited mount straight ahead, Roberts's keen eyes spotted the figures moving behind the thick, hastily-constructed barricade. Experience told him that these were Cheyenne braves he was observing. As his weary brain fought desperately to try and work out exactly what they were hoping to achieve by building

111

something his horses and wagons could quite easily crush underfoot, he noticed something to the right of his galloping mount.

A small campfire glowed at the foot of the tree line, tended by countless Cheyenne. As Roberts spotted the men beyond the wall of brush rushing towards the fire, he began to realize what they were doing. The Indians knew that no mere wall of brush could prevent his men escaping the valley, but something else could.

Suddenly, Major Roberts knew he was right. Dozens of arrows were dipped into the flames of the fire and then sent arching through the cool, night air at the makeshift obstacle.

Each and every one of the deadly fiery missiles seemed to land in the barricade before others joined them. Soon the entire length of the obstruction was alight. The wall of fire stretched from one side of the valley to the next, sending flames raging high into the sky.

The barricade had become a vicious wall of fire.

Major Thomas Roberts dragged his reins up and slowed his pace until he and Sergeant Walker were level with the following wagons and cavalrymen.

'What's going on?' Bull Fergis screamed from the driver's seat of his wagon. 'Where the hell did that fire come from?'

Major Roberts raised his left hand until each and every one of his caravan had seen his white gauntlet. Within twenty yards, they had all stopped.

Every eye watched the flames as they twisted into the night sky above them. Choking smoke swirled around the valley as the officer turned his horse and rode up beside the wagon of the frantic Fergis.

'It seems that the Cheyenne intend to try and stop our leaving their valley, Mr Fergis,' Roberts said, as he rested a hand on the long brake pole of the wagon and looked up at the started expression of the gold miner.

'We gonna stay here?' Fergis asked as he clung to the heavy leather reins and held his team of oxen in check. "Cos if'n we do, I don't reckon much on our chances, Major.'

'Nor do I,' Roberts said, as even from the distance of a quarter mile, he could feel the heat of the fire touching his controlled features.

Sergeant Walker drew his mount level. 'They got us penned in, sir.'

'How high do you think that barricade is, John?' Thomas Roberts asked as he rubbed at his dry mouth with his gloved fingers.

'Ten or twenty feet high, sir,' Walker spat as the taste of the smoke filled his mouth.

'No. Not the flames. The actual body of the barricade. How tall would you say it is?' Roberts asked.

Sergeant Walker spun his horse around and

113

looked hard at the flames before them. It was difficult to see into the heart of the fire, but not impossible

'Three feet? Maybe six.'

Roberts nodded. It's hard to tell at this distance, isn't it?' he said quietly as he allowed his mount to walk along the team of snorting oxen. 'But I have a feeling you are probably right.'

Walker allowed his horse to follow his superior officer. 'Yeah. It is kinda hard to work out how high that kindling is from here, sir. It can't be very high though. Them Cheyenne wouldn't have had time to build nothing too tall.'

'Perhaps we ought to get a tad closer?' Roberts suggested as he studied the wall of fire with an intensity few men could match. 'I think it might prove interesting, John.'

Walker swallowed hard. He knew exactly what Major Roberts meant. He had ridden with this brave soldier for too many years not to be able to read his every thought.

'Reckon you're right, sir.'

'What you two talking about?' Bull Fergis shouted at the pair of cavalrymen.

Roberts turned his head and looked back at the bearded miner whose face, like everyone else's, was illuminated in the eerie flames before them.

'Have you ever managed to get this team up to a gallop, Mr Fergis?'

'Nope. But then, I ain't ever had call to try. What you getting at, Major?' Bull Fergis asked.

'When I give the word, I want you miners to whip your teams of oxen up into a frenzy,' Roberts responded. 'I want them scared and ready to run. I want you to drive these beasts like you have never done before.'

'Why?' Fergis's voice had lost much of its power.

'Because we're going to attempt to ride straight through that wall of fire, Mr Fergis.' Thomas Roberts touched the brim of his hat before returning his attention to the flames.

'But that's suicidal,' Fergis gasped.

'Staying here is suicidal, Mr Fergis. How long do you imagine those Cheyenne braves are going to wait before they attack?'

Fergis gave a huge sigh. 'OK. You're in command. I think it's plumb *loco* but I guess we ain't got us a heap of choices.'

'Correct,' Thomas Roberts agreed.

'You figure we can get through that fire, sir?' Walker asked nervously.

'Hopefully.' Roberts lifted his canteen to his mouth and drank heartily as if for the last time. In his heart, he knew it might just be his final drink.

It took only a few minutes for the burly sergeant to ride around the hundred mounted troopers and tell them what they were going to have to do. Each man had enough time to wet their whistles and dowse their horses' heads from their canteens.

Then they saw Major Thomas Roberts lifting his white gauntlet in the air as he readied his mount for action.

It might have been the drumming of the Cheyenne that echoed around the ten wagons and the hundred waiting riders. It could have also been the combined beating of one hundred and sixty hearts that filled their ears. Whatever it was, it seemed as if every man under the command of the straight-backed officer could hear something as they waited.

As the defiant flames licked at the dark sky, each man watched the white gauntlet as it hovered above the officer's head. Then Major Roberts brought it down and spurred his horse.

It was like the start of a chariot race from ancient times as the entire troop of cavalry drove their mounts after their leader. The miners cracked their bullwhips frantically above the horns of their teams of oxen and got their vehicles moving once again.

They had not gone more than a hundred yards when the sound of arrows leaving bows filled the night air. As the riders and wagons tore across the lush valley ground through the tall, swaying grass towards the wall of fire, they saw the flaming arrows falling into their midst.

Now they were the target for the flame-tipped Cheyenne arrows – a target which the expert marksmen had little trouble locating.

Major Roberts heard the pitiful screams behind his mount as he galloped toward the flames ahead. There was no time to pause and look back. No time to fret about those who followed his charging horse. All he could do was continue leading the way towards the fire that blocked their escape. He knew that to hesitate for even a second could mean disaster.

Another wave of arrows took to the air. Then another.

Roberts slapped his reins from one side of his horse's neck to the other, lowering his head until the brim of his hat obscured the terrifying inferno ahead.

He was asking his faithful mount to do something no horse would ever willingly do, unless forced. He was asking it to ride straight into a wall of fire – the one thing that brought terror to all of God's creatures. Yet there was no alternative. The safety of the prairie lay beyond the flames and he had to try and lead the way to that objective.

Yet Roberts knew in his heart that even the bravest of mounts would more than likely refuse to cross that barricade of blazing kindling, and throw its master into or over the terrifying obstacle.

117

But he had to try. He had to attempt the impossible and lead his followers through it and hopefully on to safety.

Then a hundred fire arrows landed directly in the path of his racing horse. To the officer's amazement and gratitude the gallant horse obeyed its master and rode straight over them and crashed into the blazing wall.

Roberts felt his uniform burning as he thundered on. Looking over his shoulder, the major saw Sergeant Walker racing through the gap he had left in the burning obstruction. Within seconds he heard the sound of heavy wagons driving through the small gap he had created in the barricade. Twisting around in his saddle, the officer watched as his troopers followed.

None of his caravan of followers slowed up their pace until they had finally reached the dusty prairie, and could no longer hear the sound of Cheyenne braves' screams ringing in their ears.

Roberts stared at what was left of his command and knew he had lost many of them to the accurate bowmanship of the Indians. The wagons that had managed to escape showed all the signs of being in a battle. Half the oxen teams were skewered with arrows and the canvas tops had burned off the metal loops.

Sergeant Walker dismounted and started counting the troopers.

118

'Seventy three, John,' Major Roberts said as he slid from his saddle and sat on the hard ground holding his reins in shaking hands.

'Only seventy-three of our boys made it, sir?' Walker gasped as he stopped beside his exhausted superior.

Roberts nodded solemnly.

There were no more words from either man. There was nothing either could say.

NINETEEN

The pair of very different hunters who ascended stealthily through the thousands of straight trees could not be heard by neither man nor beast. Theirs was a skill honed through necessity to a razor-sharp edge. Iron Eyes knew he was about to do what he did best, and take the life of the vermin that had attempted to kill him and Silent Wolf.

The young Cheyenne had never hunted anything except game before, yet he too felt something stirring deep within him as he trailed the taller figure.

Someone had tried to kill them and without the intervention of Iron Eyes, might have succeeded. Silent Wolf owed the bounty hunter his life, and to a Cheyenne, it was a debt he knew that he was duty-bound to honour.

A hundred questions filtered through the

120

youth's mind as they continued climbing upward. To Iron Eyes, however, there were no questions. For this was what he had become: either the dispenser of justice or the victim of its lethal vengeance.

Somewhere up there in the forest of countless trees, there were men who had tried to kill either his companion or himself. Iron Eyes knew that it must be he who was the target. He had killed so many Wanted men during his life as a bounty hunter. Each victim had either a father, brother or son who could and would seek retribution given half a chance.

The bullets were meant for him. Only him. Iron Eyes was certain of that one simple fact. The Indian who moved alongside him had no enemies. He was still pure like the forest which surrounded them. His soul had not yet been tainted by the evil of the outside world.

As the bounty hunter screwed up his eyes and clutched one of his prized Navy Colts in his bony hand, he knew this was a mission he should be venturing into alone.

Glancing back into the face of the handsome brave who moved like himself, unheard by anyone or anything, Iron Eyes wondered whether it was true that Silent Wolf could actually turn into a wolf. The weary bounty hunter knew it was impossible for a man to change form, but there was something about the Indian that was special.

Then Iron Eyes's thoughts sharpened once again on to the job in hand. Whoever had opened up on the pair high up in the clearing, wanted only his blood. Iron Eyes gritted his razor-sharp teeth and knew that whatever lay ahead of them, they would meet it together.

However much Iron Eyes wanted to meet his fate alone, Silent Wolf was too naive to realize that the gaunt figure in the long coat beside him needed no help.

Death had ridden on the skeletal figure's shoulder for his entire life. It was the only companion Iron Eyes knew would never desert him; it would always be there, waiting for the moment when it was his time to meet the Grim Reaper. Death was the only thing Iron Eyes had ever been able to rely upon.

The three Creedy brothers had reached the clearing from which they had seen the two riders flee. Bob Creedy vainly searched for signs that their bullets had found their marks on the hard ground, as his brothers sat atop their mounts clutching their pistols.

'Any blood, Bob?' Frankie asked his older brother.

'Nope,' Bob Creedy replied, as his keen hearing told him that there were others moving around in the darkness of the heavily-wooded area that surrounded them. 'You hear that?'

Treat chewed on the butt of an unlit cigar and looked around the clearing nervously. 'Yeah, I heard something,' he replied.

Bob indicated that they should dismount. His brothers did so hurriedly and led their mounts towards some shadows.

'How many?' Frankie asked, as he tied the reins of their three horses to a stout tree trunk and knelt beside his crouching brothers.

'Hush up,' Treat demanded.

Bob raised a finger to his slips and strained to listen to the faint movements he knew were heading in their direction. He was no hunter like others who roamed this forest. He, like all the Creedys, was a killer and a thief.

'Over there!' Treat pointed.

Bob nodded. 'Aim true, boys. I figure we just found old Iron Eyes.'

They raised their weaponry and aimed in the direction of the sound, which was coming closer. They did not have to wait very long.

Bob Creedy was first to spot the glinting rifle barrel as the light of the large moon overhead bounced off it. Without a second's hesitation he raised both his guns and fired across the clearing at the waiting figures.

Treat Creedy squeezed his trigger with an

almost reluctant pain etched on his face. He had
never been the best of shots and he knew it. Even
aiming with the greatest of care, his bullets could
go anywhere.

It was the young Frankie Creedy who allowed
his weapons to do their worst, as always. It was
said that he could shoot the wings off a bumble-
bee at fifty paces. As he emptied his guns in the
direction Bob was firing, he cursed continually. Of
all the outlaw brothers, Frankie loved killing
men.

The Creedys paused for a moment to allow the
gunsmoke to drift off the high mountain clearing.
They speedily reloaded their weapons and waited
until they could see their targets once more.

Suddenly a screaming figure broke through the
heavy brush opposite them and charged across
the clearing. They could see the long, black hair
flapping on their attacker's shoulders as the
figure began cocking and firing his repeating rifle.

'Iron Eyes!' Treat Creedy exclaimed as he
stared wide-eyed at the man who was racing
straight at them.

Bullets bounced off the tree trunks around the
kneeling brothers as they were startled into firing
again. Frankie managed to hit the yelling man in
the leg as he leapt on to them.

As Bob Creedy forced the figure off Frankie
with every ounce of his strength, he saw another

man charging them. He too had a mane of long, black hair.

The smoke from the man's rifle seemed to create a fog within the clearing. A fog none of their eyes could penetrate.

Smashing the barrel of his pistol across the head of the man who was wrestling with his brothers, Bob felt the heat of hot lead as it tore through his sleeve.

Raising his guns in the rough direction he had last seen the second man, he fired. Before Bob could cock his hammers and squeeze his triggers again, the dark-haired man hit him square on.

Bob Creedy felt as if all the air had been kicked out of his body. Falling backward with the sturdy figure on top of him, he hit the ground.

Even in the smoke-filled clearing he could see the face above him. This was not Iron Eyes, he thought. Grabbing hold of the rifle barrel he fought the man for his very life on the cold soil. This was an Indian.

Seeing a knife appear in the brave's other hand, Bob Creedy grabbed at it whilst his brothers tried desperately to pull the strong Cheyenne off him.

The blade drew closer to Bob's face as the single-minded warrior bore down on him. A bullet then exploded above them both and the Indian's head shattered apart.

Blood and gore splattered over Bob Creedy as

125

the dead Cheyenne fell limply on to his prostrate form. Struggling free of the heavy weight, Bob looked into the face of Frankie who was smiling as he blew down the barrel of his pistol.

'I got the bastard, Bob.' Frankie began to laugh in a way which chilled even his brothers' blood.

Wiping the remnants of the Indian brave's brains off his face, Bob Creedy began to rise to his feet. He was only halfway up when his eyes widened at the sight behind both his brothers.

This Cheyenne brave was neither screaming nor firing a rifle as he approached. This Indian was carrying a long war lance as he ran at them.

'Frankie! Treat! Behind you!' Bob Creedy yelled as the running man got closer.

Before the two brothers could turn, the warrior reached them. His lance went straight into the middle of Treat's back and tore its way out of the front of his shirt. Frankie began to raise his guns, but felt his jaw cracking as the Cheyenne brave smashed the back of his left hand into it.

Bob Creedy picked up his pistols off the ground and pulled back both gun hammers faster than he had ever done before. He pulled the triggers without even aiming, but his bullets found their target and he watched the warrior spinning on his heels before collapsing into the dense brush.

'Treat,' Bob said as he grabbed the shoulders of his stunned brother, who was somehow still on his

126

feet with the long, lethal lance skewered through him.

Treat Creedy licked his lips silently before looking at the face of his older brother.

'This don't feel good, Bob,' Treat said as blood trickled from his mouth and dripped onto his bandanna.

'It don't look too handsome either, Treat,' Bob said as his eyes frantically tried to work out if the war lance might have missed all the vital organs. The blood-covered metal point of the lance had gone through Treat's shoulder blade and protruded a few inches below his right collarbone. It had missed the heart, but Bob knew that it must have gone through the middle of Treat's right lung.

'Which one's Iron Eyes, Bob?' Treat asked as blood flowed from his mouth, and he stumbled into the arms of his brothers.

'None of them,' Bob replied. 'They're just redskins. Iron Eyes ain't nowhere to be seen.'

'Injuns?' Treat shook his head sorrowfully. He had hoped one of the bodies lying at their feet would have been the bounty hunter who had killed Dan back in the stinking town of Bonny. That would have at least been something to take to his grave. The satisfaction that they had managed to reap vengeance.

'Yep. Just some of them Cheyenne critters the

old sheriff told us about,' Bob added.

Treat smiled. It was a gruesome sight to see a mouthful of teeth stained with so much blood and lung tissue.

'I got myself killed by a stinking Cheyenne. That ain't even funny, Bob.'

'You ain't dead yet, Treat,' Bob insisted. 'All we gotta do is pull out that lance.'

'It'll leave a mighty big hole, Bob.' Treat spat out a huge blood clot as he arched in pain.

'I'll plug up the hole, Treat. However big it is,' the eldest Creedy vowed. 'You ain't gonna die up here on this damn mountain.'

'How do you feel? Does it hurt?' Frankie asked as he supported Treat whilst Bob checked the wound carefully.

'I'm kinda short of breath, boys.' Blood dripped from Treat Creedy's mouth with every word. 'I feel like I'm drowning.'

Bob Creedy would do anything to try and save his brother's life, yet he knew that Treat was drowning.

Drowning in his own blood.

TWENTY

Iron Eyes and Silent Wolf reached the clearing roughly twenty minutes after having heard the last weapon being fired in the short but deadly gunfight. Using every shadow within the dense forest of tall pine trees, they edged their way around the clearing until they were convinced that there was no living soul inside its moonlit parameter.

Cautiously they moved into the moonlight and tried to work out what had occurred here, and why. Steam was still rising from the bodies in the brush near where the Creedys had fought the Cheyenne.

After hearing the raging gun-battle only minutes earlier, both Iron Eyes and Silent Wolf were surprised by the silence which now filled this place. They had expected to find the white men who had shot at them, but there were none to be seen.

129

Iron Eyes sniffed at the cold, night air as he
ventured forward towards the centre of the clearing. The air was still tainted with the acrid smell
of gunpowder and death. It was an aroma he had
long been used to.

The bounty hunter stared at the rising steam
which emanated from the three corpses and
pointed them out to his companion. The bodies of
the three Cheyenne braves told the two hunters
everything. The men who had tried to kill Iron
Eyes had somehow found themselves in a fight
with these Indians.

'White men,' Silent Wolf said staring at the
ground and the high-heeled-boot prints beside the
tracks of three horses.

'Shod horses?' Iron Eyes questioned.

'And much blood,' the young Cheyenne added.

'Much blood, huh?' Iron Eyes felt himself smile
as he repeated his companion's words. 'At least
your brother Cheyenne managed to wound one of
the varmints.'

Silent Wolf nodded and then pointed towards a
narrow gap in the trees.

'They go down that trail. Three men.'

The tall bounty hunter narrowed his eyes as he
glared in the direction his companion was pointing. Whoever they were, they were heading deeper
into the reservation, he thought. Were they
insane? Maybe they were just ignorant of the fact

that down there, in the belly of the reservation, there were thousands of Cheyenne. Maybe they were just plain dumb.

'It don't figure,' Iron Eyes sighed.

'Iron Eyes. Look,' Silent Wolf said picking up the blood-covered war lance, which had been broken into two pieces. 'This why white man hurt.'

Iron Eyes turned and stared at the lance in the hands of Silent Wolf before stepping closer. 'So one of them varmints got himself stuck like a pig, little hunter?'

'Much blood,' Silent Wolf said again as he tossed the war lance away and rubbed his blood-smeared hands down his buckskin shirt front. 'Men take hurt one with them.'

'Good. The bastard will leave us a nice easy trail to follow if he keeps bleeding.' Iron Eyes strolled to where the three dead Indians were lying. His eyes narrowed as he stared down at the trio of bodies.

They had been killed all right, but not cleanly the way he would have done it. There was a panic in the way these men had been killed.

'Are these men hunters like you, Silent Wolf?'

'No. They scouts. They make fire for signals to warn of danger,' Silent Wolf replied.

Iron Eyes rammed his pistol into his belt and walked towards the edge of the trail taken by the Creedys'. It was black and untouched by the moon. Silent Wolf moved to the side of the tall, gaunt figure.

'They foolish. They go wrong way. That way mean death to white men.'

Iron Eyes's head turned slowly as he absorbed the words. 'Would your people kill me if I go down there?'

'Not if you with Silent Wolf,' the young warrior said coldly.

'What if we gets separated?' Iron Eyes pulled a cigar out of his pocket and placed it between his teeth.

'Then Cheyenne might try and kill you, my friend,' Silent Wolf said.

'That sounds like bad medicine.'

'Heap bad medicine.'

Iron Eyes struck a match with his thumb nail and dragged its flame into the black cigar. Smoke drifted from his teeth whilst he began nodding.

'Reckon I better stick close to you, if I want to stay alive long enough to see morning, Silent Wolf.'

'Silent Wolf will never leave Iron Eyes. Me owe you my life.'

'Go and get our horses, little hunter. We got us some prey to catch,' Iron Eyes whispered.

TWENTY-ONE

These were young Cheyenne warriors who had tasted the blood of their mortal enemies for the first time. They had triumphed and destroyed the troopers and the gold miners who had not been able to follow Major Thomas Roberts through the wall of fire and back on to the relative safety of distant prairie.

The glory of war had returned to the hearts of the braves who had managed to trap the invaders in the narrow valley. To the majority of them, it was a new experience.

Having dispatched the last of the soldiers and the miners the same way that their fathers had done to other enemies a generation before, the younger braves seemed almost drunk with the brutal power of it all. Victory tasted good, but not as good as the barrels of hard liquor they had discovered in the captured wagons before setting the vehicles alight.

133

Now more than a hundred of the Cheyenne warriors were drinking and dancing around the blazing wagons and the mutilated bodies of their victims. Primed by the rotgut whiskey, they soon found themselves fuelled by something far more dangerous than any of them had experienced before. To them, battles were something they had only heard spoken about around the campfires by their elders. Now the taste of blood filled their souls and poisoned their judgement.

They wanted more.

Iron Eyes allowed his younger companion to lead the way down into the darkness of the steep trail. Both knew this had been where the white riders had fled after the fight back in the mountain clearing, because they had left tracks that even a blind man could follow. Branches were broken where the shoulders of the three mounted outlaws had ridden on their frantic journey down into the unknown. To the pair of experienced hunters, it was the easiest tracking either of them had ever encountered. Only the lack of light slowed Silent Wolf, yet even in the blackness of a place that the moonlight could not penetrate, the pair of expert hunters saw every sign left by the Creedy brothers.

It was almost as if they wanted to be caught, Iron Eyes thought, as he teased the reins of his tall horse. This was too easy. Far too easy.

The grey pony walked slowly down the dark trail, as its master sat gripping on to its mane. Silent Wolf's keen senses missed nothing as he steered the animal along the trail. Iron Eyes allowed his more nervous mount to follow.

This was not his land. It belonged to Silent Wolf and his tribe. He had never hunted men through terrain such as this, and knew every tree posed the threat of an ambush. With one hand on his reins and the other on the grip of one of his Navy Colts, the bounty hunter's eyes darted from one side of the trail to the other.

Iron Eyes knew he should have somehow managed to persuade Silent Wolf to hunt these ruthless killers alone, yet to do so would have put him at the mercy of the entire Cheyenne nation.

Silent Wolf was his lifeline. However much it stuck in Iron Eye's craw, he knew he needed the handsome brave, if only to stay alive long enough to get out of this hauntingly beautiful reservation.

Iron Eyes touched his scalp for the first time in hours. It hurt, but had stopped bleeding again. His head no longer ached and the only drumming he could now hear was coming from down in the heart of the forest.

They had been riding for no more than ten minutes when the young hunter dragged his crude reins and pony's mane back. The grey gelding stopped.

135

Silently, Iron Eyes moved his horse to the side of the pony and then halted. 'What is it?'

'There!' Silent Wolf pointed through the thicket of trees to a point forty or so feet below them. A place where the moonlight had found a gap in the dense tree-canopies above them.

Iron Eyes stood in his stirrups and squinted. Gradually his eyes managed to focus on the exact point his companion was pointing at. 'That's them, little hunter.'

Silent Wolf pulled his ancient rifle up from where it hung in the bag across the grey pony's shoulders. 'We shoot them now?'

Iron Eyes shook his head and pushed the barrel of the rifle down. 'Nope. Not from here. We ain't got a clean shot from this distance, little hunter.'

'Too many trees?' Silent Wolf asked as he thought about his actions more clearly.

'Yep.' Iron Eyes dismounted and tethered his reins to a stout branch. 'I got to get closer.'

Silent Wolf swiftly leapt from the back of his pony and landed beside the gruesome-featured man.

'We go.'

Iron Eyes gripped the shoulders of the smaller figure. 'Nope. I go down there alone. This ain't your fight, it's mine. You stay here where it's safe, little hunter.'

Silent Wolf was about to argue when he felt the

136

strength of Iron Eyes's hands squeezing his shoulders. Suddenly he knew the tall, rawboned figure meant it.

Reluctantly, the Cheyenne youth bowed his head in obedient frustration. 'I come if there is trouble, Iron Eyes.'

Iron Eyes smiled. 'OK. If I get myself in a fix, you come and help me.'

After patting Silent Wolf on his shoulder, Iron Eyes studied the winding trail before them. Then he stared through the trees down the steep incline filled with straight tree-trunks. He knew to take the safer route on foot would cost him far too much time. Time he could not afford. The direct path was dangerous but also one that would give him the element of surprise. Glancing at the face of Silent Wolf he nodded, and then slipped into the undergrowth and began heading down towards where he could just make out the three figures.

He knew he could have stuck to the less hazardous trail used by the riders, but instinctively felt that it would have taken too long. He had to cut down through the steep, wooded slope if he were to take these men.

The slope was slippery underfoot and the long legs of the bounty hunter seemed ill-suited to the difficult terrain. Yet he persevered on down to where the moon illuminated his prey.

Using the straight, slim trees to stop himself
from falling off the mountainside, Iron Eyes knew
whoever the three men were, they would not
expect anyone to drop in on their makeshift camp
from this deadly direction.

Halfway down, Iron Eyes had to muster every
ounce of his waning strength just to remain
upright. Leaning against the trunk of one of the
many trees he had encountered on his descent,
Iron Eyes peered down on the men.

Screwing up his eyes, the infamous figure
suddenly began to notice that this greasy, sloping
incline was not as he had first suspected when he
had started down through the trees. Now he could
make out a ledge between where he had stopped
to catch his breath, and the three figures. Iron
Eyes began to wonder how high the ledge was
from the flat ground below it. Ten feet? Maybe
twenty?

However big the drop was, Iron Eyes knew he
had to take even more care on the final part of his
descent. The last thing he wanted to do was to fall
and break his neck after surviving the slippery
slope.

Iron Eyes saw the men more clearly when he
moved down to the next tree and rested against
its trunk. Two of them were tending the injuries
of the third. For a moment Iron Eyes wondered
why they were bothering. Even at this distance

and elevation, the bounty hunter could see that
the figure was more dead than alive.

Having never had any kin himself, Iron Eyes
knew nothing of the bond between siblings. The
Creedys might have been ruthless killers and
thieves, but they were also brothers. Brothers
refused to write one another off until the very last
breath had left their bodies. To Iron Eyes it
seemed totally pointless.

The ground beneath his feet was covered in
moss, and seemed to defy anyone or anything
standing on it. Licking his dry lips, Iron Eyes
knew that unless he was extremely cautious, he
would more than likely lose his footing and fall.

Looking at his mule-ear boots, the bounty
hunter wondered if his vicious spurs might help
him from sliding down the moist, muddy slope, if
he tried to use them as an anchor. Pushing
himself from the tree, he edged away from it and
looked down at the next similar pine about ten
feet below him. Iron Eyes knew that if he could
reach that tree, he had a chance.

Jabbing the spur on his right boot backwards
into the wet ground, Iron Eyes cautiously moved
his left foot from the trunk of the tree he had been
balanced against. Then it happened.

Without knowing how, Iron Eyes felt himself
falling on to his back heavily. As his skull cracked
on to the wet ground he felt his entire body

moving quickly downward. His long coat beneath his lightweight frame offered no resistance.

Sliding helplessly down at a speed which increased with every passing heartbeat, Iron Eyes could see the moon above him through the black canopy of the pine tree branches.

Desperately, Iron Eyes clawed at the soft soil to either side of him, feeling the heat of friction beneath his spine as he continued thundering down towards the rim of the ledge he had noticed a few seconds earlier.

Raising his head to look at his boots, Iron Eyes felt a strange sensation racing through him.

As his body slid off the side of the steep mountain, he realized he was flying through the air straight at the trio of men below.

For the first time in his entire life, Iron Eyes felt fear.

TWENTY-TWO

It was the noise above them that first alerted the Creedy brothers. They had never heard anything quite like it before. It was a sound which defied definition, and caused the men to look upward.

The sight that matched the noise made little sense either to the weary minds of the outlaws. For what seemed an eternity, they watched in awe as the black shape seemed to float in the air above them. Even in the brilliant light of the large moon, their eyes refused to believe what they saw. The flapping coat tails of the bounty hunter gave the impression of a massive, winged creature as Iron Eyes's helpless form flew through the air over them.

Frankie Creedy was first to rise to his feet and draw his weapons, as the horrific vision flew over their heads like a gigantic bat. The outlaw began firing in terror as the ghostly apparition disappeared into the brush below them. For the first time since he had handled guns, Frankie had not hit what he was aiming at.

Bob Creedy jumped up and grabbed his brother's right arm as the younger man fired his last shots.

'Easy, Frankie,' Bob said whilst he raced to the edge of the slope where Iron Eyes had disappeared.

'What was it?' Frankie screamed as his shaking hands tried to empty the spent shells from his guns.

'Hush up,' Bob ordered. He vainly tried to see or hear anything from below them in the tangled brush.

Somehow Treat Creedy managed to drag his body off the cold ground and stagger to the side of his younger brother. Even with a hole in him he was still refusing to die.

'I told you this place was haunted, Frankie,' he spluttered as blood trickled from his mouth. 'This whole damn place is full of demons. That weren't no real critter.'

'Ghost?' Frankie swallowed hard.

'Or something just as evil,' Treat nodded.

Bob Creedy stared into the dense undergrowth below him, as his thumb traced over his gun hammer poking up from his right holster. He was trying to be rational and work out what he and his brothers had just witnessed, but there seemed to be no rational explanation that fitted.

'Did you see where it went, boys?'

Frankie seemed to drop more bullets on to the ground than his shaking fingers managed to get into the hot chambers of his guns when he stepped forward.

'Treat's right, Bob, It was a ghost or something. I ain't gonna stick around here and try to kill things that can't be killed.'

'There ain't no such animal as a ghost, Frankie,' Bob snapped as he felt sweat rolling freely down his face from beneath his hatband. 'Treat's fevered up. Don't pay him no heed.'

Treat hobbled closer to his elder. 'Then what was it, Bob? It weren't no owl. Was it an eagle? Mighty big, if it was.'

'I only caught a glimpse of it, Treat,' Bob replied.

'Maybe it was a flying bear?' Treat rubbed the blood from his chin and smiled. 'What was it?'

Bob Creedy turned and looked at his brothers. They looked almost as scared as he felt. 'Looked like a bat or an eagle to me. But like you said, it was kinda big.'

Frankie snapped the chamber shut on one pistol and gripped it tightly in his hand as he holstered the other. 'We better ride out of this damn place, Bob. Now.'

'The boy's right, Bob,' Treat agreed.

Bob could not see anything down below them and returned to the sides of his brothers. 'You're right. Let's ride. This place ain't natural.'

The three Creedys had no sooner mounted their spent horses when they heard the sound of a rider coming down the trail they had used to reach this very spot.

'Hear that?' Frankie asked as he drew both his guns from their holsters and cocked their hammers.

'Somebody coming real fast by the sound of it,' Bob said as his fingers gripped around his pistol and slid it out of its holster.

Treat Creedy had his work cut out for him just remaining balanced on his skittish mount. All his bloodshot eyes could do was watch the dark trail until the rider finally appeared in the moonlight.

Silent Wolf dragged back on the mane of his grey pony and then screamed a bone-chilling call at the heavens above them.

The Creedys held their horses in check as they watched the young Cheyenne before them.

'Not more damn Injuns,' Treat groaned as he watched his brothers allow their horses to advance slightly towards the handsome Indian.

'Is he alone?' Frankie asked Bob desperately as the thought of being attacked by an entire war-party crossed his mind.

Bob rested his gun on his saddle horn and studied Silent Wolf carefully. 'It's just a kid, Frankie. A little runt of a kid.'

Frankie began to smile as he raised his guns. 'Must be the left-overs from the Injuns we killed up the mountain, Bob.'

'Kill him, boy,' Bob ordered.

Frankie did not require telling twice. He brought both his arms up until they were at eye-level. As his sweating fingers curled around the triggers of his weaponry, a sound came from behind them.

Something was moving down in the brush where the ghostly apparition had vanished.

'What was that, Bob?' Frankie's voice asked in a pitch far higher than his usual tone.

Before Bob Creedy could reply to his younger brother, Silent Wolf gave an ear-piercing shriek and began to gallop straight at the three riders.

'The Injun, Frankie. He's coming at us,' Bob yelled at his distracted brother.

Frankie turned his mount full-circle and fired both his pistols at the charging Silent Wolf.

The wounded grey pony reared up on to its back legs and kicked out its hoofs in the air. Then, as Frankie fired both his guns again, the doomed animal made the most hideous noise and began bucking until its master was thrown next to the edge of the sheer drop.

Silent Wolf dragged his tomahawk from his belt

as he staggered to his feet, and threw it at the three mounted men.

As the lethal axe flew through the cold air, a volley of bullets were blasted at the young Cheyenne. The ground at his feet tore up as the bullets hit the soil, making Silent Wolf move backwards.

It was a scream only fatally-wounded men can make. The tomahawk hit Treat Creedy in the centre of his face and drove his weakened body over the cantle of his saddle, until it fell in a lifeless heap on the ground.

'Treat!' Frankie screamed.

'He's gone this time, boy,' Bob yelled pointing at Silent Wolf. 'Let's get him.'

At that very moment behind the Creedys, a dishevelled figure managed to claw his way out of the brush. Iron Eyes's head was filled with the thunderous explosions again. He could hear nothing except the drumming of his own heartbeat as it pounded inside his skull.

As he staggered upright, Iron Eyes saw the two men shooting at Silent Wolf, forcing him back to the very rim of the ledge.

Dragging one of his Navy Colts from his belt, Iron Eyes raised the gun and fired.

Startled, the pair of riders drove their horses straight at Silent Wolf.

Iron Eyes could not tell which of the riders

kicked the young Cheyenne hunter as they made their escape. All he knew for certain was that Silent Wolf had fallen into the black abyss below and the killers had fled.

When he reached the spot where he had seen Silent Wolf fall, Iron Eyes clenched his fists in fury.

'I'll get them, little hunter. I'll make them pay,' he vowed as he stared down at a million trees.

As each sinew in his battered body cursed his every movement, Iron Eyes somehow managed to run across the moonlit clearing and grab the reins of the mount belonging to the fallen Treat Creedy. Dragging the long leathers into his bleeding hands, the bounty hunter pulled the animal close, before stepping into the stirrup and mounting the horse.

This was now personal.

Few people managed to penetrate the armour-like defences of this ruthless hunter of men, but Silent Wolf had managed it without even trying.

Hauling the reins hard to his side, Iron Eyes thrust his long, vicious spurs into the trail-weary mount and forced it to a gallop up the muddy rise into the darkness of the trail.

With the keen instincts that had been honed over a lifetime of killing for survival, Iron Eyes knew exactly which direction his prey had taken in their attempt to escape his wrath. Even in the blackness of a trail that he had never ridden before Iron Eyes knew where they had headed.

Forcing the creature beneath his spurs to find a speed that was ill-suited to such an overgrown trail, the injured rider drove on and on.

Whoever these men were ahead of his mount, they were already dead as far as the lethal killing-machine was concerned. There was no escape from Iron Eyes. No man had ever escaped the venom of the cruel rider when he had the scent of the kill in his narrow nostrils. No one could find a rock large enough to hide beneath to save their bacon when he was after them.

Ascending the steep trail atop the nervous mount, Iron Eyes knew he was returning to the place where he and his companion Silent Wolf had found the bodies of the three Cheyenne – the spot where these unknown whites had shot at them.

Reaching the halfway point on the dark trail, his deadly eyes spotted the outline of his own horse standing where he had tethered it only minutes earlier.

Dragging his reins up to his chest, Iron Eyes paused for a mere few seconds whilst he transferred from the Creedy horse to his own rested mount. Pulling the razor-sharp Bowie knife from his right boot, Iron Eyes cut through the reins at the tree branch. There was no time to untie knots. No time for a moment's hesitation. He had to ride on after the vermin who had killed his young friend.

With a relatively fresh horse beneath him, Iron Eyes had to catch up with the two unknown riders and dispatch his own branch of vengeance upon them.

Driving the tall horse up the trail by whipping it with what was left of the reins and stabbing its flesh with the spurs he always used mercilessly, Iron Eyes began to hear the sound of horses ahead of him. For the first time since he had staggered up out of the brush where he had landed after flying over the heads of the Creedys, Iron Eyes could actually hear something apart from the noises inside his head.

Forcing his mount on, Iron Eyes spotted the tails of the two horsemen ahead of him, as they reached the high clearing. Within a few dozen yards of the moonlit area, Iron Eyes threw his leg over the neck of his galloping mount and dropped to the ground. He watched his tall horse continue on up into the clearing, and then heard the deafening noise of gunfire.

As the bounty hunter moved with the pair of matched Navy Colts in his bony hands, he watched his mount being cut to ribbons by the bullets of his enemies.

Continuing to the very edge of the clearing, Iron Eyes cocked the hammers back on his pistols until they fully locked. He had no fear within him now, for this was the moment of judgement – the moment all skilled hunters trained themselves to face when they had located their prey.

To a creature such as Iron Eyes, it made no difference what the prey was. Whether it was a rabbit to fill his belly or a man whose value had been decreed by the law, it made no difference at all.

Reaching the moonlight, the battle-scarred figure glanced all around the clearing with a unique determination. He saw his fallen horse still kicking at the air as death slowly over-whelmed it. The air was still thick with the black gunsmoke of the two Creedy brothers' pistols.

Iron Eyes knew that they were scared. They had unleashed every bullet from their two pairs of Remingtons and Colts when his horse had ridden into the moonlight, without even waiting to see whether it had a rider.

Gritting his small sharp teeth, Iron Eyes knelt and studied the area before him – a place it seemed death had claimed for its own.

For a few endless seconds his keen vision saw nothing of the two men he sought. Only the evidence of their lethal actions in the form of his fatally-wounded mount and the three bodies of the Cheyenne braves.

Then he suddenly realized that the dead

Indians' corpses were now stacked like a wall, and not strewn apart as they had been when he and Silent Wolf had discovered them. If the two men were anywhere at all, they were hiding behind the hastily-constructed barricade of bodies, he thought.

Screwing his eyes up even more than usual, the bounty hunter tried to seek out their hidden mounts. His eyes might not have been able to locate them, but his hearing told him that they were tied up somewhere beyond the bodies of the Cheyenne. Somewhere in the darkness of the forest.

Moving on to his belly, Iron Eyes began to crawl towards his stricken horse. There was little cover in the high, bright clearing apart from his horse which lay on its side twenty or so feet ahead of him.

Reaching the prostrate creature, Iron Eyes dropped both his Navy Colts into his coat pockets and pulled his Winchester out from its saddle scabbard before trying to cock its stiff mechanism.

This was a weapon he seldom used, and it showed. If ever a rifle was in need of attention, it was this one, but he had no time to rebuke himself. Now he had to avenge the young Cheyenne hunter called Silent Wolf. Nothing else mattered.

Digging deep inside the pockets of his coat, he

managed to find a few rifle shells amongst the dozens of pistol bullets.

Forcing the three bullets into the carbine and cranking its rusty lever, Iron Eyes began to wonder who these men that he wanted to kill so desperately actually were.

The thought did not have time to take root in his mind. A swarm of bullets volleyed across the clearing and ripped into the body of the horse, forcing the bounty hunter to duck behind its massive bulk.

Rolling over until he could see beneath the neck of the dead animal, Iron Eyes carefully aimed the Winchester at the two gunmen he could see firing at him.

Squeezing the trigger of the Winchester was easy. Getting it to fire was another matter. The trigger seemed to jam halfway through its action.

'Damn!' Iron Eyes cursed as he angrily tossed the rifle away and began to reach in his pocket for the pair of trusty Navy Colts.

Bob Creedy must have had the eyes of an eagle, for he spotted the form of the bounty hunter just behind the twisted neck of the horse. It was only a half-chance, but that was all he knew his brother needed. Pointing, Bob handed his own fully-loaded Winchester to Frankie.

'That must be Iron Eyes, boy. Kill him.'

Frankie raised the rifle to his shoulder and

quickly adjusted the sights before squeezing its trigger. This carbine was unlike the one that the bounty hunter had tried to use. This one was greased and cleaned to perfection.

The bullet exploded from the long barrel of Creedy's rifle, and would have gone straight through the skull of Iron Eyes had the bounty hunter not raised one of his Navy Colts a fraction of a second before the lead ball reached its target.

Iron Eyes felt an agonizing pain as the gun was torn from his grip and smashed into his face by the sheer force of the accurate bullet.

The pain of the pistol hitting his face had been bad enough for the bounty hunter, but the white flash of swirling fog inside his head came as a total shock. With blood pouring from his face, Iron Eyes battled vainly to cling on to consciousness, but he knew he had failed when his head fell back into the damp grass. Suddenly, every one of the honed senses that he possessed in abundance deserted him. Iron Eyes was out cold.

'You got him!' Bob Creedy screamed in delight. 'You killed the famed Iron Eyes, Frankie!'

Both men cautiously got to their feet. They began to advance towards the figure who was lying outstretched beyond the dead horse. Even now, the Creedys knew they were not safe. No man of Iron Eyes's reputation could be so easily dismissed.

Frankie cocked the rifle again and kept it trained on the motionless figure as they drew closer, his elder brother keeping both his pistols on Iron Eyes.

'Is he dead?' Bob asked as they circled the neck of the horse hesitantly.

Frankie stared at the face of Iron Eyes – a face covered in blood caused by the impact of the Navy Colt.

'Looks like I got the varmint straight between the eyes, Bob.'

Bob Creedy began to grin. 'What a shot, boy. What a shot. Even old Dan could not have made such a shot.'

Both men stood over the still figure and laughed at the sight of their handiwork. Had they done the impossible? Had they killed the man, who, it was said, could not be killed?

Both the Navy Colts were yards away from the thick hands of the bounty hunter. This was no trick, they both thought. Iron Eyes was dead.

'We ought to empty our guns into him, Frankie,' Bob suggested.

'Why? I already done for him.'

'For Dan and Treat, boy. And maybe just for fun.' Bob Creedy slowly aimed the barrels of his pistols at the blood-covered face of Iron Eyes.

Before Frankie had time to reply or lift the Winchester up to his shoulder, the sound of a howling wolf filled their ears as it bayed at the large moon. The creature was close.

Both brothers spun on their heels and frantically glanced around the clearing. Then they saw it.

'A wolf!' Frankie gasped as the handsome animal walked steadily towards them. The yellow pupils of its eyes seemed fixed on the outlaws as it approached.

'Easy, boy,' said Bob Creedy as he tried to control his shaking hands and aim at the advancing creature.

The wolf shook its head and bared its fangs. The growl was something neither man had ever heard before. It was far louder than they had imagined it could possibly be.

The animal continued walking towards the Creedys as Iron Eyes blinked behind them and focused on the two figures. Rolling over unnoticed, the bounty hunter was about to reach for one of his Navy Colts when he too saw the wolf.

'Kill it, boy. Kill that critter,' Bob demanded.

Both men began to fire their weaponry with a mixture of fear and desperation. It was as if the sound of thunder filled the mountain clearing. The acrid gunsmoke soon blurred their vision, but the sound of the wolf continued.

No amount of bullets seemed able to stop the advance of the growling wolf. Then it struck.

Iron Eyes managed to crawl to the closest of his pistols, and lay with his back against the saddle of his fallen horse. The black smoke of so many gun and rifle shots masked his eyes from seeing the men vainly trying to fend off the wolf, but he heard every sound.

The jaws of the raging animal ripped and tore at the Creedy brothers. Their pitiful screams chilled even Iron Eyes.

Then it went silent.

FINALE

Iron Eyes waited like a condemned man until the black smoke finally drifted off the side of the mountain and he could see the carnage before him. Swallowing hard, he stared at the proud wolf who stood a mere twenty feet from him beside the bodies of the Creedy brothers.

Iron Eyes used his coat sleeve to wipe the blood from his face and gripped his gun tightly, whilst the wolf slowly began to walk through the wet grass towards him. Was it now his turn to be torn apart by the blood-covered fangs? He rested the Navy Colt on his leg and continued staring into the eyes of the approaching wolf.

Then his mind was filled with the memory of the face of young Silent Wolf. As the creature drew ever closer to the seated Iron Eyes, he noticed that the animal was not growling as it had done with the two outlaws.

For some reason that even he could not understand, Iron Eyes released his grip on the pistol and allowed it to slide off his leg into the grass beside him.

The animal stopped beside the blood-stained boots of Iron Eyes and began panting. The yellow eyes of the wolf fixed on to those of the injured bounty hunter.

'Little hunter?' Iron Eyes heard himself say.

The wolf bowed its handsome head, turned and disappeared into the mist, which was rising from the grass as the first rays of the sun began to warm a new day.

It took the bounty hunter less than an hour to do what he had to do.

Riding one of the mounts left by the savaged Creedy brothers, Iron Eyes headed back along the trail he had used to enter the forest. The other horse was laden down with what was left of the two outlaws. If they had a price on their heads, he was going to claim it.

Reaching the hot prairie, Iron Eyes aimed the horse towards the distant town of Bonny.

Tapping his spurs into the flesh of the mount, Iron Eyes could hear the howling of a wolf coming from the highest point of the tree-covered mountains behind him.

He did not turn to look.

Iron Eyes knew exactly what Silent Wolf looked like.